EBENEZER

JoSelle Vanderhooft

ZUMAYA BOUNDLESS   **AUSTIN TX**

2013

EBENEZER

© 2013 by JoSelle Vanderhooft

ISBN 978-1-61271-068-6

Cover art and design © Vince Trancgyvier

"Zumaya Boundless" and the eagle logo are trademarks of Zumaya Publications LLC, Austin TX.

Look for us online at
http://www.zumayapublications.com

Library of Congress Cataloging-in-Publication Data

Vanderhooft, JoSelle.
  Ebenezer / Joselle Vanderhooft.
    pages cm
  ISBN 978-1-61271-068-6 (print/trade pbk. : alk. paper) — ISBN 978-1-61271-069-3 (electronic/ multiple format) (print) — ISBN 978-1-61271-070-9 (electronic/epub) (print)
  1. Young women—Fiction. 2. New York (N.Y.)—Fiction. 3. Christmas stories. I. Title.
  PS3622.A5925E24 2012
  813'.6—dc23
                                    2012037659

For Kim, as ever

PROLOGUE

Marley was dead.

Not dead as doornails or coffin-nails, although it made little difference. Her boxes had been closed with long brown stripes of packing tape, her velvet sofa and zebra-gaudy beanbags loaded into the back of a We-Haul-It van, her dishes stacked in glistening bubble wrap, her shower caddy plucked from its customary nest between the haphazard shampoo bottles and crumbling soap bars in the mildewed shower.

She had even removed the drooping aloe from the windowsill where its stalks had hung brown and useless like the legs of a dead spider. How you could kill such a hardy desert plant, Ebenezer could not have said, but it must have taken diligence, time, concerted effort.

The metaphor and its attendant irony were not lost on her.

Marley was dead, and snow was falling like static. Ebenezer watched it from a couch warmed only by a laptop. The ancient radiator hummed uncertainly; a pipe banged like an aneurysm somewhere deep within the chipped walls. Her index finger had left a smear of oil on the touchpad.

No call, no email, no text message, no whisper, and no tweet. A month, the calendar insisted, each black X a little tombstone. A month, and Ebenezer sat staring at the dust in which the sofa's outline vanished a little more every time she looked.

How did one measure time, she wondered. In seconds, or the dark spaces between them? In the hours that tumbled past like snowflakes, or in their weight on her shoulders. The clock ticked steadily with the storm's pattern. Ebenezer glanced over at its nook. Seven-thirty. Seven days exactly. It could well have been seven years.

Marley was dead—to her, anyway.

The alarm shrieked through the silence, assuming once again that she had gone to bed. Ebenezer sighed and hit it. Christmas Eve morning.

What did she have to show for it?

Act I

Cold Was Cheap

Scene I

An Excellent Woman of Business

Ebenezer was a small woman, five-foot-four and frail as newspaper against December. The snow blasting down 94th and West End made her walk at angles and huddle deeply in her coat—torn, dirt-flecked and handed down like a family history of depression, it had seen far better days. Cabs were too expensive, subways and buses too close; and Ebenezer had a fear of all those bodies, and the eyes placed in them. The streets being no less populous but far more open, she walked each day to her collections job—rain, shine, gale or, in this case, ice blizzard.

The wind ripped through her mud-brown hair, even the babies' fists of tangles, and squinted her already slitted gray eyes even further in a face the color of winter itself. Her scarf fluttered uselessly, half off her narrow shoulder, half hanging down her chest. She had lost her fifth pair of street-stall gloves last week and could not budget for or bother about a sixth, her rent not being controlled and rumbling to increase after the new year.

She was shivering all the time, and something bad was following her.

Ebenezer could not have said just what it was, save that it felt like a breeze beneath her collar, prickling when it should have tickled. That it resembled ripples in the corners of her sight that resolved to quiet air when she turned her head. It was as if night had come down cold and three hours early and brought with it the full weights of the planets. A heaviness had stalked her now for years, weighting down her arms and dragging at her ankles, transmogrifying everything to leaden chill. Some days, even rising from bed and walking to the kitchenette felt like dragging three miles of iron chains.

Today, those miles felt to Ebenezer as though they had elongated well past five. As New York City rumbled past beneath the gathering clouds, she felt slow and clumsy—if an accidental elbow or an ill-placed foot were to send her sprawling, she doubted she would rise until sometime past spring.

A breath of winter blasted through the streets, rumpling Ebenezer's maxi-coat up to her shins and overwhelming her with the smells of cold sidewalks and construction, bodega daisies, car exhaust, and, oh, so many bodies. And something else—metallic, sharp as the there-but-not-quite bite of ozone.

Something flickered again at the edges of her vision—pale as mold spots, linked like manacles. Ebenezer's heart kicked against her back. She turned...

Only the gray street looked back at her.

She rubbed her temples, blinking. Stay here. Stay together, damn it.

4

The feeling came again, as if someone were staring at the back of her head. She sighed. Merry Christmas.

She snorted, troubling the head cold she had been fighting off since Thanksgiving. Fuck it all.

Ebenezer worked in a frequently re-purposed office between a condemned mission that flooded in every rainstorm, and a Thai restaurant specializing as much in water-stained carpets and plastic tiger lilies as it did in peanut sauce. The windows were a bit too clean and whole for this stretch of 51st Street.

Here, five times a week for six hours a day, Ebenezer sat sandwiched between the bare slate walls of a cubical, hitting the keys of an equally nondescript computer that, while too clean, was not particularly modern.

After punching into this beige-carpeted farm, she hung her tattered coat and scarf in a colorless break room where the Pepsi machine perpetually displayed an out-of-order sign. Her arms goose-pimpled and her nipples shriveled underneath her fleece sweater as she entered the floor. Coats—especially coats as unsightly as hers—were forbidden in the office, yet the thermostat never seemed to rise above 40 save for during the summer months.

As she walked her chair up to her desk, Ebenezer shivered and mulled upon her theories with a scowl— a broken heater, a cheap landlord, or a boss who simply did not care, each translated into greed and disregard, and the holiday needed no help in being worse.

As she eased into the rickety computer chair, the heaviness persisted. The thought of sitting silently and allowing it to pull her down through the gruel-gray

5

carpet was the most alluring notion she'd had in days. But it was five past ten, and the computer needed fingers to make it dial, a voice to give the task a point. Ebenezer slipped the headset over her hair and with it, a resolved: A part. The only one you'll play. So, play it well.

The women to either side had not said hello. True, Ebenezer knew no more of them than Left's blond perm and Right's black comb coils, but she still felt angry at their silence.

She brought up her call list and, as she did five days a week for six hours each day, transported that feeling into her work. In this she found her four years of acting school, the loans for which still pendulumed over her, more useful than the breathing exercises and the near-psychotic dissociation her more sensitive coworkers used to get them through the afternoon.

Like all those beneath the perforated ceiling tiles, Ebenezer's business was misfortune—debts medical and, therefore, as unavoidable as they were unpayable. Many on her list today seemed to understand the mathematics; machine after machine recorded her monotone request for a call back and the helpful 800 number. Some rang and rang into a telling silence; others were picked up on annoyance, sometimes rage.

How dare you, you fucking bitch? I don't have it! Stop calling me! another wailed before the dial tone filled her headset. *Christmas Eve!* they said with one outraged voice. *Christmas Eve, Ebenezer! Have a heart!*

But I can't, Ebenezer told herself as one woman wept down into silence. It was an expense she could not cover if rent and groceries were to be paid, an expense she could not cover and go on. They, of all people, should understand, she thought as she cut short a call that was spiraling into a death threat shot through with shards of misogyny. Like every other part of life, a job had a script, and it had to be followed, even if the words were sharp and felt wrong in your mouth.

As for its being Christmas Eve, well, what did they expect? Your debt doesn't take holidays, she thought, and promptly filed the remark in the ledgers of her mind for later use.

Her fingers chattered briefly on the keys, nails the purple of a fresh bruise. She knew her intrusions were less welcome than those of a politician scrabbling for a vote or a chirpy recording selling sham car insurance. But humanity was just as much her business as it was for these other callers.

A knock on the cubicle's rim, and her supervisor's chubby face appeared, followed shortly by the rest of him. Despite his knotted hair and the sweat perpetually pearling on his shale-colored skin, Fred Carter was a Santa Claus of a man who seemed to have misplaced his sleigh and reindeer and a good deal of his mirth. Still, he was much better than his bosses Trent and Cindy, who made a fine art out of glares and veiled threats.

He stepped in as far as his girth and polite distance would permit and wiped his forehead on his sleeve. How he could sweat in this polar office was anybody's guess and gossip.

"All right there, Ebenezer?"

Ebenezer had crafted a smile and a response for such occasions. She showed both now—"Doing great, thanks!" followed by two rows of teeth.

Fred, however, sometimes had a *Miracle on 34th Street* gift for seeing through bullshit. As he edged in farther, Ebenezer suspected now was one such time.

"I just wanted to thank you for working Christmas Eve," he started with all that Utah Mormon charm Ebenezer suspected got him mugged regularly in Manhattan, not to mention mocked by his ward members. "We really appreciate your help."

Somehow, she doubted Carker & Tulkinghorn really did. And how a guy who said things like "appreciate" and "thank you" got into debt collection in the first place she couldn't fathom.

"It's no problem," she said, hoping through her smile that three sentences would make an end of it.

But Fred leaned against the filing cabinet as if settling down for a mug of hot chocolate.

"And I just wanted to let you know that it's all right! Everybody's numbers have been down this month. It's just that time of year, not you."

Except it was, and they both knew it, as did her paycheck. As did her rent and every ramen package on her counter. As did Marley, seven somethings gone and disappointed.

Ebenezer's smile, however, had a staying power all its own.

"Yeah, I know. But all I can do is try my best, right?" That seemed to be the spell for banishment.

Just like that, Fred leaned closer and dropped the bullshit, too.

"Ebenezer, I really mean it. Sometimes it's just a bad month. And that's what I wrote in the evaluation." He looked left-right, as if he had farted. "You do good work.

Real good. You're an asset to the shift. I said that, too. Just so you know."

He smiled and reached out as if to touch her shoulder, and then withdrew his hand back to his pocket.

Ebenezer felt like she had just ingested a lump of charcoal. Of course, she should have known this was coming, she thought. Twenty closed cases in November and only fifteen so far this month. Of course she should have known. Of course she would be told today.

It's Christmas Eve, Ebenezer! twenty debtors chorused in her head.

And then, the Santa-smile returned, Fred was pressing a mauve-and-teal-striped candy cane into her hand.

"I brought them special for the afternoon shift." His hand traveled to his brow again, and Ebenezer immediately thought better of unwrapping the treat. "Try not to let it get you down, okay? It'll all work out. You have a merry Christmas."

"Merry Christmas," she replied, as if a key had been wound, a mechanism tripped.

Then, as awkwardly as he had come, Fred Carter waddled off to deliver more glad tidings to the shift, more promises of firings not to come, more hideous buck-a-dozen sweets.

Ebenezer dropped hers in the wire trashcan and returned to her call list. Merry Christmas. Fuck it all. She punched the scroll button as if it were at fault.

Martha Cratchit was the next name, and Ebenezer groaned as she dialed. Of all the people on her list, Cratchit had to be the least creative and, therefore, the most frustrating. Each day since December first the same excuse—*I don't have it.* No embellishments, no begging, no stories changing fast as salmon leaping through bright water.

Ebenezer was already in a foul mood, and as she punched in the last two digits, she decided her patience had run out.

The receiver was picked up on the second ring; Cratchit was also apparently too stupid to invest in caller ID.

"Hello?"

The blistering, just-been-slapped whine was definitely hers. Ebenezer immediately felt her anger rise.

"Ma'am, this is Ebenezer calling from Carker and Tulkinghorn. Yet again."

Cratchit sighed. Ebenezer imagined a bonbon of a woman in a muumuu and housecoat, skin like melting wax, pinching the bridge of her bulbous nose.

"You people just don't stop. It's Christmas Eve!"

"No shit, really? Too bad your debt doesn't take a vacation."

She heard shuffling, as if Cratchit were pushing through a pile of newspapers.

"This is real inconvenient. My kids are—"

"And I'm sure they'd love to know all about how you mismanage your money."

"And I told you people not to call me—"

"There's no law against—"

"—at home. I know my rights."

"Then you know there's no law against calling people who owe money."

"I tell you, I can't pay now. What's the point of calling?"

10

"Because, uh, you owe my client? Are you that fucking stupid?"

"Look, I'm not working now. I'm sick. I got diabetes and a heart—"

"Well, at least that's some new excuses." Ebenezer looked down at her fingernails. One had broken between home and work. Shit.

"—which you know all about, since that's the reason I have these bills." Cratchit sighed, and again Ebenezer imagined the bulbous nose, the large fingers scissoring the bridge. "Don't call me again. I'll pay when I can, and that's the best I can do."

"Well, ma'am, the best you can do sucks!" Ebenezer bit her nail, twisting off the excess. "Not that it matters, though. I'm calling the police, and when I do, they'll issue a warrant for your arrest."

Cratchit tried to start several sentences at once, each ending in a squawk.

"It's Christmas Eve!" she kept repeating.

"Like that means anything. You're eight months past due and no payments, not even interest. That means you'll serve two hundred days, minimum."

Again several half-born sentences.

"I'm *sick*," Cratchit protested at last. "I'm sick. I'm on insulin, ACEs, and two things for depression. I tell you, I can't work and I can't pay now!"

"Well, ma'am, then I really hope you like prison. That's where you're going if you don't pay your bill."

Of course, it was all nonsense—yesterday Ebenezer had told one man she had a court order; the day before, she'd threatened to call one office worker's boss. But while she had to stay within the law's bounds—

11

well, story-telling sometimes got results from the ig-
norant or easily cowed.

Cratchit apparently was both. Now she was making a sound like down pillows might make if they could
cry.

"I've got two little kids…" Ebenezer thought she
heard her say.

"Whatever. Pay your debts or get off my fucking
phone."

The tears flowed freely then, and Ebenezer imagined the leakings of that bulbous proboscis with a shudder.

"I'll pay you when I can. Stop calling me. I mean it."

A click. The dial tone like a tomb's echo.

Ebenezer ended the call and sighed.

"And a very Merry Christmas to you, too."

She thought she saw a flash of Left's blond hair
peeking over the cubicle's rim, but when she looked,
she only saw a cluster of ornaments hung up last week
in some useless attempt to make the cube farm festive.
Shrugging, Ebenezer scrolled to the next name.

Six hours passed like the growth of glaciers. There were
more hang-ups, more machines, more ringing into silence, and many not-at-homes. Of those who answered,
four cried openly, five swore like cabbies, and two actually made plans to pay. Well, two more for her record,
Ebenezer thought as she clocked out with not so much
as a glance from anyone in the farm.

Outside, the snow had not let up a bit, but at least
the street was somewhat warmer than the office. Tired

of her cold apartment and its waiting shelves of instant noodles, she blew into a sad McDonalds and splurged on a cheeseburger, chicken nuggets, French fries and, a little worried about her bleeding gums, a heaping salad. The bill was not quite too much for her ever-reducing salary; still, the coming rent bump meant even fast food would be a luxury before spring.

But she could pay her bills. There was always temp work, waitressing. Maybe a commercial…

But Ebenezer shook the thought away as she pulled at her soda. The audition lines were long enough even at non-paying companies, and even they had stopped calling. Everybody had a resumé, a talent, a dream dropped from twelve stories. The cube farm had taught her that much. This Christmas Eve was bad enough without over-thinking.

Her hands felt like two locked safes as she bagged the cheeseburger for later and stepped out again. It was only five o'clock, but the storm made everything look darker, stranger. Snow, fog, and gloom sat heavy among the ropes of tinsel and gave the Christmas lights wrapped around the bare branches such a sinister cast Ebenezer could well understand why they were sometimes known as "fairy lights."

The weather shrouded the higher stories and distorted the Salvation Army bells. Even the scents of sugared almonds, coffee, and hot chocolate were faint, frosted with chill and ozone and the mélange of asphalt, granite, dirt, and sewer that was every New York street. At every side on Ebenezer's path, people raced the weather, clutching great bright packages and sacks of fruit and sweets, or floral arrangements protected by puffs of plastic. Everyone seemed to be going some-where and nowhere at once, a separate species bound on journeys she could not follow.

For awhile, she struggled through the crowds, look-ing for distraction and excuses not to return to her apartment and its many ghosts, but the coffee shops and stores overflowed and the bars and restaurants cost too much. Eventually, the heavy numbness and boredom drove her back to her building's cracked steps and bro-ken elevator.

Twisting her key in the stubborn lock, Ebenezer paused, listening for the familiar sounds of running water and the television's hum—the Discovery chan-nel or something. Her favorite. She could almost hear the actors' voices—*could* hear them!

The lock clicked, and she hoped—a misunderstand-ing, a bad dream; it had to be.

The door swung in on darkness. Still and empty, as she'd left it, the dust outlines of furniture still scar-ring the floors. The answering machine flashed like a cyborg's eye, the only sign of life here.

The first caller ID showed a Utah number—her mother, who would only want to offer money Ebe-nezer knew she did not have and words she did not want to hear.

The next was an obvious telemarketer. Then Bell, inviting her to some dreadful Christmas party for the fifteenth time and asking her to "hang out," the tone of her voice long past annoying. Ebenezer deleted each without listening then poured herself the final glass of red wine from the bottle Marley had generously for-gotten.

She tried to watch the television, but its five channels were all families, warm apple cider, and second chances. After the fifth angel seeking his wings and the fifteenth Christmas carol, Ebenezer found the shopping network and let it run for noise.

The bed was currently a mess of laundry, books, and all the disarray of a relationship cut off. Even had it been made and its sheets fresh, Ebenezer had no desire to sleep there. Again she curled up on the ratty love seat that had followed her from Salt Lake City. The blankets—also Marley's leavings—still smelled like her, and roses. As she had done for seven days or seven years, Ebenezer forbade herself to cry, but the pillow still felt damp. *Marley*, she remembered. *Marley*.

Marley crouched at their—at *the*—tiny stove, triumphant over dill-sauced salmon, dumplings, sweet potato pone, the whole wide culinary world.

Marley at the television, cursing one president out and weeping another in.

Marley in thigh socks and a negligee, waiting for Ebenezer to find a vase for a dozen Valentine's Day red roses.

Marley's skin—lampshade-pale and freckled, from an Irish mother, she'd explained on their second date.

Marley taking her first taste of sashimi, her bony fingers graceful and expert with the porcelain chopsticks, the laughing O of her red lips. The way they had kissed and kissed after, in the cab, and then in the bed that became theirs.

Marley looking on empty space with all its scuffs and blank walls and pronouncing it "the perfect place."

Marley red-eyed and keeping her words as close as tax forms.

Marley, her face blotched like a globe, half-sore with shouting. *Yes, that's the problem, Ebenezer! You don't talk! You never tell me anything, goddamn it!*

Marley's lips firm as a minus sign seven days or seven years or seven centuries ago, the flatline of her voice. *Don't call. Not now. Maybe not ever. I don't know.*

I don't know.

Over and over, Ebenezer turned these memories like stones. Again they became a carousel of light and sound and the smell of every rose. She turned and turned, half sleeping, half-awake, but all certain.

Marley was dead as doornails, door locks, dusty corners, dank streets, dark theaters, and debt, debt, debt. Dead as the city murmuring with Christmas-time yet unaware its great heart had stopped.

"It wasn't supposed to be like this," Ebenezer told the silence. "None of it."

The unseen weights hung low and heavy on her limbs. Outside the window panes, snow fell like knives.

Act II

The First of the
Three Spirits

Scene I

Bear But a Touch of My Hand Here Upon Your Heart

It wasn't supposed to be like this.

Ebenezer knew all too well how everything should have been. She had written out the plan and repeated it nightly, a prayer to a god who seemed far less certain than ambition. Work hard up through university, star in every play, study and train and one day— one day, someone will notice and say, "You! Yes, you! I want you. You just shine so brightly."

Ebenezer had been waiting to be seen for twenty-nine years. With thirty just around the corner, in all its sag and loneliness, her prayers were more fevered than ever, and her sleeps more fitful—more like reveries, in fact.

The carousel of light and memory turned her round and round and touched her down at last in the dark living room.

Dark?

Ebenezer blinked and turned her head. The television's eye looked back at her, striped gray-and-orange from the lamps outside, where the snow was still coming down like static.

Strange. She shifted the quilts away, shivering as her toes touched the chilly floor. Kneeling, she rattled the power button and frowned when the set did not respond. She checked the plug, still tight within the socket, and the DVD player's clock—00:00. No light peeked beneath the front door, and the windows in the building across the alley were all dark and still. A power failure on the entire block?

"But why are the streetlights on?" she said out loud. "How long have I been asleep?"

The snow fell so fast and the storm was so fierce, it could have been fifteen minutes or five hours. Her nose pressed against the glass as she searched the streets for vehicles and passers-by, counting a minute out by way of Mississippi. Sixty seconds passed, then sixty more. Nothing rustled past but gale-blown snow, not even a newspaper or haphazard trash bag.

She felt a chill that had nothing to do with the gasping, ancient radiator.

"What the hell is going on?"

The smell of sweet sage tickled her throat. A hint at first—no more, perhaps, than a trick of memory. Confused, Ebenezer looked away from the alleys below and sniffed the air. Faint, but yes, desert sage, then rabbit brush, cottonwoods, sharp juniper berries, and over all—over all—noon on red sand and striated sediment.

A cold, wet feeling prickled in her wrists, and she turned slowly, as if knee-deep in dreaming. She wasn't sure she was not.

18

Darkness crept behind her, restless down the walls like hair falling and falling, a shiver under every door—bedroom, entrance, and bath. In the latter, a crawling in the pipes like the legs of some great millipede.

Horror clawing in her chest, she staggered to the window and the amber glow of streetlights beyond as plaster grains pelted the toilet, the range top, the barren hardwood floors. A skittering overhead; her eyes turned upwards, where the ceiling distended like a stomach upon which great seams of night spread like veins. Darkness trickled softly from them.

Something rustled in her hair and scampered down her face; Ebenezer ripped at it, screaming loud enough, she hoped, to wake up.

Her fingers scrabbled against sand.

She held one shaking hand aloft to catch some then rolled it in her palm. Yes, sand, and as near as she could tell, sand red as rust. She brought it to her nose and sniffed—hot.

It slithered from her palm and into the great pile accumulating in the center of the floor. Fed by tributaries from all parts of the apartment, it vaguely resembled—Ebenezer squinted—a stone pillar?

In the bathroom, the light fixtures smashed to the floor with a sound like wings and bones. Ebenezer found her courage and grabbed on tight.

"Whoever…whatever you are, stop it! Stop it now!"

Just like that, the sandfall did. And, just like that, the street lamps all snuffed out. A chuckle, rich and low as earth, cut short her second scream.

"My, my, Ebenezer. Seven years out, and you've forgotten me so easily?"

Ebenezer's voice sputtered and collapsed. The lights kicked on again, high and bright as the parcans above a stage. Sure enough, these fixtures hung like beetles above her. She squinted, finding herself the object of a spotlight. Beyond its circumference, the apartment had vanished save for the column, which glowed even redder now in the theatrical light.

Now I know I'm dreaming.

Hesitant as a sleeper, she stepped from the spot-lit circle and edged toward the construct. She stalked around it like a vulture, studying each fissure and cranny with an actor's attention. She knew the story about a pinch being enough to startle someone from a nightmare, but having dreamed of many pinches, she decided another kind of touch was necessary. She brushed two fingers across the pillar, found it cool and smooth from erosion.

The stone moved with a sound like a shifting fault line, and Ebenezer jumped back as if scalded, only half aware the follow spot had found her once again. A woman now stood in the pillar's place—or something like a woman.

As Ebenezer stared, the light on the stranger shifted to a pleasing honey glow. Her hair was a tangle of sage and tumbleweeds with cactus blossoms, morning glories, and the occasional wagon wheel and chrome fender caught up in its whorls. Her body was a study in red-veined sandstone and the bones of dinosaurs, polished, sleek, and naked as noon. Ebenezer blushed away from pebbled nipples and taut belly, turning her gaze instead to the blue-sky eyes.

"You know who I am," the sandstone woman said.

20

Ebenezer knew the answer in her bones.

"Utah," she whispered.

"Its genius, yes." The desert-woman smiled, her mouth full of sego lily petals. Her laugh was as warm and rich as her scent, which engulfed Ebenezer like a weather system.

"But…" she stammered. "How…?"

The desert-woman held aloft one lime-striped hand.

"You spent your summers wandering though my valleys, and your winters saddened by the white death enshrouding me. You hiked along my spine and picked sparkling rocks from my hair. As you slept, I soothed you with cricket song and stars, and when you wept, my hand lay always on your head." Utah looked at her with eyes as clear as mountain streams. "I heard you. Even across this blinking continent, I heard you. And I came."

Ebenezer's mouth closed, opened, closed. She briefly envisioned Martha Cratchit then shooed away the image.

"But why…?"

One finger grazed her cheek, and it was rough and warm and so very red.

"You often looked into my eyes and showed me hope. But now your face is thin, and want is written on your brow in ash."

"I remember," Ebenezer looked away. "If this is a dream, it's a sad one." *Like everything*, she wanted to add, but it sounded like bad melodrama.

"Not all sad," the Genius of Utah said as if she had heard anyway. Her tumbleweed hair shifted as she lowered one great hand. "Come with me."

"Where?" she asked suspiciously.

"Where else but home?"

Ebenezer halted in mid-step.

"It's not home anymore. Here is home now."

"And where is here, exactly?"

Ebenezer looked around the stage. At all points, it expanded into carmine shadow. She recalled the warehouse where she had performed three years past, which a now-deceased company had converted into a black box.

"I don't know," she admitted. "But it isn't *there*."

Utah smiled, and not unkindly.

"When you can't find yourself, where better to look than in the past? And home is not one place, Ebenezer. Home is your history. No matter how far you range away, you cannot forget it or divorce it. You cannot leave it behind like a candy wrapper any more than you may discard your heart and keep on walking."

"But I've left it before!" Ebenezer snapped. "And I had the best reason there is!"

"I know. I've watched you try to drop your past in a trashcan over and over, and watched you go back and pull it out again just as many times." The spirit shook her head, as if her pity were interlaced with something more. "Now, won't you come home with me? The pie is getting cold."

"What pie?"

But the heady air now swirled with the smells of pumpkin, whipped cream and allspice, and something…

Something like a Utah winter.

"My time is as long as your history," the genius said. Her voice was clear as mountain air.

Another glance at her surroundings was enough; there was no going back to her apartment. As if grasping a rattlesnake, Ebenezer took the offered hand.

The lighting shifted, and the empty theatre dissolved.

Scene II

A Clear, Cold Winter Day, With Snow Upon the Ground

Snow like icing on gingerbread roofs frosted thickly against the skeletal cottonwoods but so thinly on the lawns that the corpses of catalpa leaves peeked wetly through. Snow patched the rusty mountains like a quilt, hanging like discarded shawls off the great sandstone cliffs in the hazeless distance. The cheerful morning sun was weak as chamomile, but the air was so clear and cold it stung.

Ebenezer's flesh pimpled immediately. Rubbing her arms, she cursed.

"I don't know what happened to my apartment, but wasn't there any way for me to bring my coat?"

"Sorry." The Genius of Utah bent low as a pine bough stooped with icicles. Her body was similarly wintered; her stone was a wash of fallow and ecru, her nakedness partially hidden in hoarfrost. Her hair looked smashed and dry. "But don't worry, you'll be warm soon enough."

She straightened and walked away

"Where are you going?"

"Why don't you follow and find out?"

Standing there wouldn't get her warm, Ebenezer decided. She tagged after the stone woman, rubbing her upper arms.

"You don't understand—I hate the cold."

"Oh, yes, I do. You never did like that about me. Don't fuss, Ebenezer. History is made equally of heat and cold."

"And business casual is made for seventy degrees." Ebenezer stopped and stared. "I know this road. The cemetery on the left…" She gestured where it slept. "The canal…" A little farther on, where it sludged in half-hibernation. "I live—I *lived* just down the street from here. But the diner…that development—they're gone now. It's Vernal, but it looks like nineteen-eighty-nine again."

The genius inclined her tangled head.

"Well." Heat spread through Ebenezer's cheeks. "Well, I mean…"

She shook her head and crouched on the asphalt. Utah watched in silence as she ran her palms over it.

"It's real," she whispered.

Then she ran. If she remembered—and she knew she damn well did—it was just around the corner, past the stable and Mr. Jergensen's junk-strewn yard Aunt Iola called an eyesore. Her slim calves cramped, and the cold air tore at her lungs long before she reached her destination. At the chain link fence, she stopped and bowed low, wheezing for her breath.

25

"I walk every day," she gasped. "Every day, at least forty New York blocks. You'd think I…I could run… half a street."

The jovial genius was at her elbow, looking no more winded than the wind itself.

"A New York block? Is that something like a New York minute?"

Ebenezer shushed her. The little redbrick house looked so peaceful behind the skeletal lilac bushes she did not want to disturb it.

A lock of smoke curled from the chimney and unwound into the morning, as if it were waking. As they watched, the lace curtains shifted, and a round face peeked between them.

No more than eight, the little girl was pale and plump, her features British in that vague way brought about by two centuries of distance. Her hair was straight and black as basalt and all in sleepy tangles. The green eyes, though, were as lively as a Christmas morning, which Ebenezer knew this was as surely as she recognized her younger self.

"You don't need to hide," Utah said as she crouched behind the mailbox—a ridiculous position for one of such grace, Ebenezer thought. "She can't see us. No one can."

Ebenezer ran her fingers down the beard of icicles beneath the tin box and felt hot needles sting her throat.

"We're not exactly ghosts here…"

Another laugh from those gritty lips.

"It's *your* history, Ebenezer. For you, the ice is just as cold as it was twenty-two years ago. As for me…"

Her stony fingers scraped her breasts, shaking a few pebbles loose. "Well, I'm not exactly startling—she's looking at me right now, after all. Just like she does every Christmas morning."

Sure enough, the young Ebenezer was staring out, her eyes dark and glassy as they studied the scraggled lilac bush, the muddy road, the prickly fields beyond. And everywhere, everywhere, the snow, already bright enough to pain her irises—Ebenezer knew because her eyes strained with the child's. Had the snow really been so bright in those days?

The wistfulness came to her voice unbidden.

"Christmas morning was always so beautiful."

"Thank you." Utah straightened up and smiled. "But you said you were cold. Shall we?"

As fast as thought, they were inside the little house, where the living room's walls were patterned up and down with explosions of magnolias that looked very old. Although a little newer, the carpet was much the same color, and every piece of furniture, from the low end tables to the rocking chair and even the picture frames, bore a gold sheen—polished brass, Ebenezer's adult-mind concluded. Yet, it felt both proper and sumptuous.

Although the Genius of Utah had appeared as large as a white pine tree at their first meeting, she somehow managed to fit into the corner where the Christmas tree sparkled, some of its ornaments so threadbare grown Ebenezer and her child-self could not help but to assign them fanciful dates of issue.

Eighteen fifty-two, they agreed of the tattered yellow ball on a low branch.

Something fluttered in the corner of her eye. Her younger self was squirming from her perch onto the floor. There, she crawled, crab-stealthy, to the tree's underskirts, where one particularly large present stood out from the rest. Rolling onto her round stomach, she poked a chubby finger into it once, twice, before tipping it.

"Ebenezer!" From the kitchen, the thick smells of bacon, scrambled eggs, hash browns. a grandmother's voice. "You better not be shaking those presents again!"

"No, Gramma."

The girl rolled back onto her haunches with a sigh. A wax cast of a face peered around the kitchen doorway, blue eyes bright within layers of tallow. Young Ebenezer giggled and squirmed onto her knees, but the salt-and-pepper-haired woman moved faster, catching her around the waist before she could rise.

"Ah-hah! Gotcha!"

"Gramma! I wasn't shaking them!"

"I wasn't shaking them! I wasn't shaking them!" Ebenezer's grandmother stuck her tongue out as she rattled her descendant by the shoulders.

"Gramma! *Gramma!*"

"What? I'm not shaking you! I promise!"

This continued until the two tumbled, laughing, to the floor. Another woman stepped from the kitchen, drying her ruddy hands on her flowered apron. Like grandmother and granddaughter, her face and waist were soft and full.

She stared at them and shook her head.

"How uncouth."

But she couldn't stop the smile from breaking out as her mother hugged her only daughter. Ebenezer's future self wondered how the woman could have ever looked so happy, or so young.

"All right, Ebenezer. Time to get dressed."

The child pulled herself from Grandma's arms, a frown trembling on her lips.

"Mom, do I have to? There's presents!"

The large woman smoothed a brown curl over her ear; Ebenezer noted it was rooted in a frost-like gray.

"There *are* presents, you mean. And you can open them after you get dressed, when Auntie Vona comes."

"But that one looks really nice," the girl wheedled, looking at the big bright package with a wistfulness that made her 29-year-old self half-smile.

"Then it can be the first one you open—later." And mother wrapped daughter in a hug Ebenezer knew smelled like homemade sweet rolls, then playfully batted the little girl's behind. "Now, go on. Get the blue shirt—it's not itchy."

"Yeah, yeah."

As mother ducked back into the kitchen, grandmother nudged young Ebenezer's back with a package much smaller than its paper bow.

"Here, go open this one in your room. She won't even notice it's gone." And they shared a wink.

The tableaux was pleasant, but what of it? These Christmas scents and sights and laughter only made Ebenezer feel heavier, and gray.

"I see why you didn't want to come back now. This was obviously such a hard time for you."

"Shut up!" Her anger startled her, but not enough to apologize. "You think one good Christmas makes a fantastic fucking childhood? Do you?"

29

The genius shrugged stony shoulders, causing a pebble to dislodge. The room's corners folded up into shadows, and matriarch and child began to shrink with it.

"Any childhood's great when you're under ten and your parents don't hit you. It doesn't matter. And don't tell me it does!" she snapped as Utah's mouth opened a crack.

"I was just going to say you're sounding very spoiled now."

"And you sound like my last girlfriend."

The room wavered like bad TV reception then resolved into sneaker-pocked snow, a cold park bench, two ragged trees leaning like conspiring lovers over two young women—a red-cheeked Ebenezer, her breath pluming in the cold, standing in the same way as the trees, and a taller girl, freckled.

"I think we'd be great for each other," the other woman said. Her hair was like a wound against the sky.

Ebenezer broke the image with shout. The world swirled back into ghost rags.

"Goddamn it, I am *not* looking at that!"

"Look at what you want—it's your story," Utah said.

As Ebenezer turned to tell her off, the genius altered again. Her body was now a marbled shade of white-and-purple, like the prickly mountains in December. Where sage and weeds had tangled, pines now bloomed on the rocky scalp, and—Ebenezer noted, an uncomfortable warmth spreading through her belly—between the statuesque thighs. As she wondered at the change, she noticed her new surroundings...

Scene III

A Long and Melancholy Room

They stood on a rambling avenue where all the houses seemed to have been built before 1920; great Victorian mansions proudly propped their snowy roofs up against the bruised mountains. The sloping streets and looming foothills told Ebenezer they had come to Salt Lake City. The white towers of the Latter-day Saint temple gleamed through the stubbly trees—an unusually clear morning, she thought. She could even make out the golden statue of Moroni, stuck in eternal trumpet-blowing.

She didn't need to turn around. She could feel it at her back, watching, almost hungry. Before she could protest they were inside it, gazing at the immaculate end tables and the heliotrope-print wallpaper Ebenezer had progressively come to loathe almost as much as she had the people who had picked these furnishings out.

Now ten years old and looking far more sullen, Ebenezer perched on a love seat with what had to be an antiqued mahogany armature. Her red velvet dress looked stiff and far too young for her, and her older self well knew that it itched terribly, and the lace edging in particular.

A postcard scene—only the Christmas tree and the scores of presents with their delicate golden bows could not outshine the girl's clenched brow, the forced-back tears that made her eyes glisten like river stones.

A tall, thin woman with skin like unfired porcelain stood within slapping distance, her hair a stiff corona of bottle brown. She dangled a gaudy, glittery ornament from her fingertips.

"What. The hell. Is this?"

Young Ebenezer stared down at her mary janes.

"We made them—."

"You made them where? In retard crafts?"

Her stepmother's tone was as casual as a wasp investigating the heliotropes and irises in her garden.

"The class made them," Ebenezer pulled at the lace along one puffy sleeve. A quarter-inch tore loose.

"Don't pick at your dress!" And the sting came out. LaDonna waved the ornament as if it were a pornographic book. "You're always wrecking things."

"Sorry," the girl whispered.

If LaDonna heard, she didn't care. She was examining the ornament as she would a cockroach. It had a gaudy red ribbon for a hanger, which she flicked disdainfully.

"Do you know what's special about glitter, Ebenezer?"

Her young self did not try at an answer, and anyway, LaDonna continued without waiting for one.

"You can get it at the grocery store for a dollar a box—less than that, even. It makes everything sparkle, which makes you want to use more and more, until it gets all over everything. But that's okay. It just means that you care more, right?"

Younger Ebenezer's answer might well have been a breeze.

"I guess?"

LaDonna's smile took on an edge.

"How old are you again?"

"Ten." Even her older self had to lean in to hear the word.

"And how much does your mother give you for an allowance?"

"Fifty cents."

"And your father?"

"A dollar," younger Ebenezer said, looking just as puzzled as she felt.

"Almost eighty dollars a year."

"Mom says I'm saving for—"

LaDonna waved her explanation away.

"You spend it all on hamburgers and candy, which is why you're so fat." The bridge of her narrow nose wrinkled. "You know what Ronelle did? She saved up her money and bought us all nice things that don't leak all over the carpet I just vacuumed."

The older Ebenezer felt her shoulders clench.

"Don't try to reason with her," she urged herself, even though the scene was like a broken mirror—unfixable.

"Mom liked her hers a lot," the girl tried.

"Your mother's also teaching you bad habits, so *you* can be crazy and stupid, too. So that doesn't mean a lot."

"Mom's not crazy. She just sometimes gets sad," the girl said. The tears polished her eyes into obsidian, but she would not let them fall.

"Crazy and stupid," LaDonna repeated, as if that made it so. "Look at this!" She stabbed her toe against the carpet. "I spent all week cleaning up for company, and in five seconds, you destroy it all."

"I'm sorry!"

LaDonna shook her head.

"I tried to make you feel welcome. I made you that special pineapple Jell-O and bought you those books…" She shook her head again. "You really hate me, don't you?"

"Huh?"

"You dropped my Dresden bowl. You scratched the hardwood floor, and now…when I just vacuumed." The ornament made a sound like a falling icicle as it bounced against the hearth "Well, fine. If that's what you want, you can forget Christmas."

Younger Ebenezer stiffened as if jabbed by a cold needle, then shattered into a thing of arms and tears.

"No! Don't do that! Not that!"

"Shut up. Sit back down."

"Please don't! I'll stop breaking things, I promise! I'll sit here and be really, really quiet! You won't even know I'm here."

"Don't touch me." The woman stepped back as Ebenezer reached for her.

"Please, I'll be better! Please don't do it, Mom!"

LaDonna punched her in the face.

In her corner, Ebenezer winced as blood leaked down her girl-self's face onto the white carpet. The

34

child staggered, stunned, and touched her bleeding nose as her stepmother spoke in quiet tones.

"Don't call me that. Not ever. Do you understand?"

Her younger self could only nod like an automaton.

"You're a selfish brat, and messy. And if you don't watch it, they'll put *you* on crazy pills, too." LaDonna sighed, as if her trials were really great, and pointed at the blood and glitter. "Since you don't appreciate cleanliness, you're going to pick up every speck of glitter and wash out all this blood."

"And then you won't be mad?"

"Oh, no. We're past that now. You're going to spend the rest of the week in your room. You tried to ruin Christmas for us, so you don't get to be a part of it."

Her young self shook as she knelt and ran her fingertips over a shimmer of glitter. Ebenezer wondered how she'd managed not to collapse from the injury and the terror of it all.

"Dirty," LaDonna muttered.

Ebenezer looked at her stepmother's eyes, her silk dress with its snowflake pattern, the meretricious tree dipping with ornaments and tinsel—even at the hideous wallpaper. Anywhere but at the kitchen entrance.

It did no good; she knew who was framed in the doorway.

Neither transfixed nor casual, her father's gaze was dull as matte paper, as if he had been entranced by too much football. The girl looked to him, her mouth opening around a stillborn plea. He looked back then shuffled into the kitchen. The refrigerator snapped open, shut like a ghost. Even now, she couldn't tell if the quiet sound the plate made as it touched the table embodied her father's fear or shame or if it was, like so many things, meaningless.

Satisfied that the day would finally go as she desired, LaDonna glided into the dining room, Ebenezer presumed then, as now, to set out the bone china in exactly three place settings.

Then, and all the other times that followed, she did not permit herself a tear, nor did she now.

She did, however, turn and leave the house, and walk down the icy driveway, not caring if Utah followed.

As she reached the street, the genius stepped up beside her.

"Penny for your thoughts?"

"I'm going home. Wherever. Back to my apartment. Christmas sucks enough right now without this shit."

"Like I said, it's *your* past, and you can't—"

Ebenezer turned and stepped in front of her.

"I mean, can you tell me what the purpose of *that* was? 'Ohh, Ebenezer hasn't had enough bad luck lately? I know! Let's make her more miserable!'"

"If you saw it, then it was something you had to see," Utah said cryptically.

Ebenezer didn't know what to do. At last she settled for kicking a pile of snow.

"If you're trying to say I'm just harboring some poor, abused inner child deep down, and that's why my life sucks, shove it. It's not like that. At all." She could not deny the anger clawing in her stomach. Nonetheless, she shrugged, took five deep breaths. "A lot of children get slapped around. It isn't some great trag-

36

edy, and it doesn't make you special. I thought it did when I was twenty-two and a budding alcoholic, and after a shrink took a third of my paycheck for five months, I realized it didn't.

"LaDonna's a bitch. Ronelle's thirty-four and spends Mommy's money on crack. Dad still says they're both living saints, and I'm a thankless bitch.

"When I was sixteen, LaDonna went to hit me, and I broke her arm. None of them have forgiven me since. We don't talk anymore, and that suits us all just fine."

The genius's smile could have been whimsical or sympathetic. Snow the hue of dishwater fell across her shoulders.

Ebenezer shrugged. "Anyway, it gave me lots of shit to work with. That's the saying—actors don't get hurt, they just get material." She had tried to sound jokey, and failed spectacularly.

The genius raised one piney eyebrow politely.

"That's just the thing."

Ebenezer's forced smile failed, too.

"Yeah, well. That was my last Christmas with Lady LaDonna and the willfully comatose father. After that, I only went for summers and the holidays where libraries stayed open. Not that it mattered. She always found a way to ruin it." She kicked the snow again. "And she said *I* wrecked everything."

She turned again and stepped from the ice-clogged street into the snug Vernal living room. Utah followed, and her city skin and evergreen hair shifted back to muddy sandstone and hardy sage.

Scene IV

Home Like Heaven

"I like that look better on you. More natural," Ebenezer said, hoping the subject would change, too.

"You felt better here," the genius observed.

"Not always." Ebenezer frowned and chewed her lower lip.

"Is something wrong?"

"No. Just something Marley said to me last week— or maybe when we first met. About how I don't open up enough." She shrugged. "It's not important."

Utah inclined her shaggy head but did not press the matter as they looked upon the past again.

Now fourteen, Ebenezer lounged on the floor in a holey T-shirt and a pair of too-large sweatpants. Lazily, she dipped her toes against the tattered carpet as she turned the pages of a playscript. From time to time, she would mark her place with an index finger, scrunch up her face and whisper quietly, as if praying.

A beetle-black CD player two hours delivered from its package rested at her elbow. "As If We Never Said Goodbye" whispered from it on a third rotation.

A wheelchair squeaked from the kitchen, bearing heavyset, cloud-haired Aunt Vona in a loud, beribboned Kelly green sweater she had no doubt herself knit. The little bells sewn onto the collar tinkled, catching the teenager's attention.

"Land o' Goshen, Ebenezer! How many times have you played that?"

"Sorry, Aunt V." Ebenezer tapped the power button, cutting Glenn Close off in mid-crescendo.

Aunt Vona pulled down her brake.

"Oh, land's sakes, child. Go on and enjoy your gift! I wouldn'ta bought it if I didn't think you'd like it. Though how you read with all that noise, I'll never know."

"It's okay. I should probably be concentrating on this."

Rolling back onto her stomach, the girl reopened her yellowing paperback; her older self read *Shakespeare* in Old English lettering across the cover.

Aunt Vona grunted up from the wheelchair and down into the room's sole plush-upholstered rocker. It had been buttercup-yellow before Vietnam, and now boasted a grimy sulfurous hue.

"What are you reading for on Christmas Day?"

"It's Shakespeare, Aunt V. *Romeo and Juliet*."

The woman clicked her tongue and leaned down for her knitting bag.

"You ask me, these teachers give you kids too much homework these days."

Ebenezer put the book aside and crab-crawled to her feet.

"No, not homework. We read the play in English, but we're doing it in drama club in March. Auditions are the day after we get back."

Aunt Vona clucked again as she rolled her unfinished afghan across her lap.

"Well, I still think it's a sin to make you study on Christmas. Girl your age should be out playing with her friends, not holed up with a book."

"I don't mind," the teen insisted, looking down at the carpet. "I really don't. I mean, Shakespeare also said "the play's the thing," right?"

"Come on, child. Why don't you call up that Jensen girl, invite her over for a slumber party? All work and no play makes Jane a dull girl."

Ebenezer's neck had reddened to a shade quite past embarrassment.

"Says the aunt who spent all morning knitting," she said as she batted at a ball of violet yarn.

"Well, that's differ'nt," her great-aunt huffed before poking her in the nose with the flat end of her knitting needle. "Now, stop that, child! You're bad as the cat."

"Mroww!"

"Oh, hush yourself." The old woman chuckled, giving her niece another prod.

The older Ebenezer groaned.

"God, that fucking play. We lost the knife and the poison vial, our Lady Capulet got food poisoning, and the curtains caught on fire." She snorted. "I got cast as Balthasar, naturally, the first in a long line of disappointments."

But of course, her younger self could not know this. Ebenezer watched her as she laid her head on her aunt's knee. She seemed so enthused, so excitable. Had she really been that young once?

40

She looked at Utah, who merely smiled her desert smile.

"Is that an afghan for Aunt Adaleen?" the girl asked, peering into the floral yarn bag.

"No, Ada don't like dark colors. It's your mother's Christmas present. I'd'a had it done if I hadn't'a caught that cold."

Ebenezer snorted as she fished an unused ball of yarn from the bag.

"I don't think pneumonia's a cold, Aunt V. And anyway, Mom says it's the thought that counts."

"I reckon so, child. But your mom should have some nice things for Christmas, too."

"She says it's good you're here. And that you brought your pumpkin pie, and that Grandma's making potatoes, gravy, and stuffing. And that I'm handling the salad and the cranberry sauce and the turkey." Her grin seemed like a canyon to her older self. "Bet I can make a whole dinner from scratch real soon."

"Why, I bet the boys'll just love that!"

It would have gone unnoticed to anyone else looking on, but Ebenezer saw her younger self shift in just such a way. Her shoulders rounded slightly, as if trying to protect her viscera. Her smile became too bright, too toothy.

"Yeah, the boys."

"Aw, look at that blush! Bet you have a beau."

Young Ebenezer twined her fingers through the skein of purple yarn.

"No one."

Aunt Vona nudged her with a bubble-shaped elbow.

41

"Come on, now. Tell me."

"Auntie," the teenager complained, returning the poke as good as it was given. "There's nobody. Really. I'm too busy with school and drama club. Besides, the boys are kinda immature." She wrinkled her nose in a way Ebenezer found both familiar and endearing.

"Was I really that cute? That clueless?"

Utah's smile was all lilies, but again she gave no answers.

"Well, I reckon they look like that now, but they do grow up. When I was a bit younger'n you, I just thought Levi Evans was the most ignernt thing! He put toads in my lunchbox and threw snowballs at all the girls come winter."

Aunt Vona was rarely one for wistfulness or melancholy, except on Veterans' and Memorial days, or whenever Levi Evans came up. Ebenezer's younger self rested her head familiarly on the older woman's knees.

"He sounds like he was great."

"Well, bless your heart! He was, Ebenezer. He was. We lost too many of the good ones in that war. And you don't hear nothin' about it in the schools. And that last letter he sent me—from France of all places!"

Grateful for the distraction, her younger self folded Vona's great hand in her own frail pair.

"Hey, Auntie. Don't be sad. It's Christmas."

The sun came out again.

"You're right, mopin' don't do no good! How 'bout you stop trying to unwind my yarn, and I'll teach you what I'm doing here? If you can about cook a whole dinner from scratch, it's high time you learned how to knit a throw."

"She died when I was nineteen, just a few weeks after my birthday," Ebenezer said as the teen sat down to watch the demonstration."I never told her, either. About why I really didn't date. It would have broken her heart." She chuckled mirthlessly. "I guess that makes me guilty of internalized homophobia. Marley would love to know that." The thought made her chest feel entirely too full. "Fucking Marley."

Her mother and grandmother entered the room, diverting Ebenezer's attention from another loop of acrimony. Her grandmother's tallowy face was still faintly tanned from a summer and an autumn coaching the vegetable patch behind their ramshackle fence.

In contrast, her mother was pale to the point of tombstones, her eyes shrunken up in sick circles, her robe and nightgown baggy from a rush of lost weight.

With a stage whisper of "Aw, heck," Vona struggled to hide her knitting.

"God, she really looks bad." Ebenezer cringed. "Did she always look that bad?" But her teenaged self did not look concerned.

"Mom! You're up!" She clasped her arms around her mother's waist and squeezed—had Ebenezer truly once hugged that hard? "Are you feeling better?"

Her mother's smile looked like a smile's ghost, yet at the same time it was stronger than a house.

"A little, Ebbie. Thanks."

"Can I get you something? Some tea? You missed breakfast, but I can make some eggs or some toast or something, if you want."

Her mother settled one hand in her daughter's hair and smoothed lock after dark lock behind an ear.

"I'm not really that hungry, but tea would be nice. Grandma's got the kettle on."

"Can I, like, help you to the couch, then?"

Her mother's smile warmed just a little.

"I'm just depressed, Ebbie, my feet work fine. Although you *can* tell Vona to stop trying to shove that afghan behind the recliner."

"Well, dammit."

"Vona!" Ebenezer's grandmother cried.

"Aw, hell, Iola. We're old as dirt. Don't tell me you ain't heard a cuss now and then."

"Well, I'll clean it off, then." The teenager grabbed a plastic Sears bag and attacked the ribbons, paper and foam peanuts littering the sofa's floral cushions.

"Still, you shouldn't say that in front of Ebenezer," Iola grumbled.

"Why, I bet she hears worse things at school. Don't you, child?"

"A lot worse. Like in gym, this girl named Mary told me that her period—"

Her grandmother waved the words away like mosquitoes.

"No! I don't want to know."

"Iola, you're a hoot," Vona laughed, having completely given up on hiding the afghan. "Ebenezer, be a dear and turn on the television?"

Her mother frowned. "It's probably just *Music and the Spoken Word*."

"Land o' Goshen, that old boring thing? I was hopin' we'd find *It's a Wonderful Life*!" said Vona breezily.

All four women groaned as the set played back static, then static on every channel but the one out of

Brigham Young University, on which a stiff-tied man droned about the Christmas season and holiness.

"President Hunter looks like he just ate a box of bugs!" Ebenezer clapped her hands over her mouth. "Uh. Sorry, Aunt V. No offense."

"Well, that's nothing new," her mother said as she draped a blanket across her lap.

"Guess there's a line down," Aunt Vona observed as her sister fiddled with the rabbit ears. "It sure snowed last night. That's prob'ly what did it."

"Well, goddamn it." Iola gave the television's frame a good, hard slap. The Latter-day Saint leader's visage wavered, greened, then hazed out completely.

"What's that about language, Grandma?" Ebenezer chirped as she poked her mother in the side. And all four of them looked at one another and laughed, shattering what little ice had formed around their holiday.

"TV rots your brains anyway," Iola grumbled, hitting the tile of a power button and ending the set's misery.

Ebenezer clasped her hands and shifted, in the way she did when trying to be casual.

"Well, you know, I *am* trying out for *Romeo and Juliet*."

"That's Shakespeare, isn't it?" Iola sat down in the chair next to Vona's.

"Uh-huh. And I want Tybalt—that's Juliet's cousin—but since I could get any part, it's probably good if I know how to do them all. So how 'bout I be your TV?"

Her grandmother needed some convincing ("I read one play in high school, I think *Othello*, and I couldn't

45

understand a word."), but she gave in before shuffling off uncertainly to fetch the tea. Ebenezer's younger self cleared the remaining wrappings from the floor while bouncing anxiously from foot to foot, the only sign of being a teenager she had demonstrated so far, in her older self's opinion.

Her acting, on the other hand, was hardly so mature—breathy, mispronounced, a different voice for every character, a flute song for Juliet and a basso for Lord Capulet that made the older Ebenezer's stomach flutter with embarrassment, then rage. She tried her best to breathe, to push it firmly to the side as she did each day with all feelings but null, all whispers of anything but necessity, necessity, survive, survive.

"No wonder everybody laughs at you and slams your face into lockers—girls *and* boys. You're a self-important little virgin who thinks knowing who Samuel Beckett is makes you special," she told her former self. "Well, guess what? It doesn't. You don't belong to an LDS ward, and your mother's in the hospital in Salt Lake at least twice a year on suicide watch! You wear sweatpants in the summer. You're weird enough already!"

"Oh, then I see Queen Mab hath been with you!" younger Ebenezer cried.

"Everyone's laughing, and you're just too stupid to see it. Or too sheltered—since it's been nineteen-fifty-two in Vernal forever, and Mom won't let you do anything because she thinks you're crazy like she is!"

"Ebenezer…" Utah started.

But Ebenezer did not care to listen. She stepped in front of the girl, who declaimed quite through her.

46

"And in this state she gallops night by night,/ Through lovers' brains, and then they dream of love…"

"They're going to laugh at you at the audition, and Mr. Jensen's going to tell you not to try out for the summer play because—oh, how did he put it? 'I like having you in the club, Ebenezer, but you're just not ready yet. Sign up for Drama II, and work stage crew for *Music Man* this summer. Take lots of notes on how Tami plays Ermengarde.' You were a fucking joke to them. You're still a fucking joke."

"Sometimes she driveth o'er a soldier's neck!/And then dreams he of cutting foreign throats!"

"And you do it. Every time, no matter what they ask, no matter what they give you, and your family says, Great! Our famous actress! They line up behind you like a…like a fence, and you listen.

"LaDonna looks at you like you're a yeast infection, and your father shrugs like he always does, and you stay up reading Stanislavski so late you nearly flunk math. And when they accept you to the fancy New York school on scholarship and your mom's well enough now that you can go, you think—That's it!"

"This is that very Mab!/That plats the manes of horses in the night!"

Ebenezer's voice had risen to a shout as well.

"And the whole time, the whole goddamned time after that, you think, 'It's going to get better. Just another year, and then there's college…Just another show, and then I'll be the lead!…Just another audition and I'll get it!…Just another show, and there'll be money!'" Her hands shook; she clenched them into fists. "It's not enough. *You're* not enough!"

"This is she!"

"*It's* not enough!" With a cry like shattering ribs, Ebenezer threw herself on the girl—and passed right through her, insubstantial as her criticisms. Staggering away, she slammed her fist against the wall instead. Her knuckles scraped, but the shadow boxes did not even rattle. She felt a pain behind her eyes and wondered when the tears had started. "Self-important...stupid—I wish you were dead."

"Peace, Mercutio! Thou talkst of nothing."

And yet.

And yet, she was so beautiful.

A whisper like wind through the sage, and Utah was at her side, her large hand warm as summer dawn on Ebenezer's back. The touch stung her, and she pulled away. In the background, her young self bowed to generous applause and announced a five-minute intermission for sugar cookies.

But her voice was soft and far away, and as she exited, so did the house.

No frosty streets or snow-drooped cottonwoods met Ebenezer. Instead, a red velvet curtain engulfed her like the petals of a great tulip. It swirled up dust and the smell of ink-black coffee dregs. Blond wood floorboards spread beneath its weighted hem, which rose on the buzz of high fluorescents.

"No," she murmured. "Not this..."

Scene V

A Golden Idol

The studio was too big. Twenty of students circled their chairs at its center, as if the rehearsal furniture in the corners—black blocks and steps, and door frames opening on nowhere—had teeth and meant them harm. Each wore a variation of the sleepy, over-harried college student's uniform of jeans and sweats and free T-shirts.

All but one dark-haired girl hunched over her notebook, whose black dress and blazer would have better suited an interview than an early class. She could have only been described as rapt, and with good reason—Lydia Bradstreet had entered.

"Good morning," Lydia called as she grabbed a clunky rehearsal chair. When two girls hopped to their feet she waved them away with an "I got it, I got it." Still, she grunted in relief as she set her burden down in an empty space.

Even seen from far away and through eleven years of memory, her wide back moved stiffly, as if the vertebrae were fused. Ebenezer's neck warmed. It did not matter. Her acting teacher had the kind of grace

49

she had previously only seen in movies, from her dark-brown skin to her round eyes and the braids that were shot with gray like lightning strikes. Back then, Ebenezer was not certain whether her younger self was in love with her, or wanted to be her. Was not certain even now.

Lydia settled on the therapeutic cushion she always carried with her and stretched her arms in front of her to loosen her shoulders.

"I hope you've all been working on your audition pieces," she said, "because we're going to take a look today. You're all set for that, right?"

Some of the students nodded, none looking so very pleased as Ebenezer. Others shuffled their sneakers, guilty in the way of students who have put television or beer ahead of being responsible.

Lydia regarded them all with a little curl of a smile, the one that said *I know you* rather than *I'm going to lecture you now*.

"Mhm. That's what I thought. Here's the thing, kiddos: if Playwrights Horizons calls, they ain't gonna wait for you to dust off your Sarah Kane and Shakespeare. You'll remember that for Wednesday."

It was not a question, and they all knew it.

"Okay." Lydia settled back into the chair and crossed her heavy legs. "So, who wants to go first?"

Ebenezer's hand shot up; her older self knew she had been waiting for that question.

"Ebenezer." Lydia nodded and indicated the center of the circle with a wave of her hand. "Floor's yours."

"Haven't I seen enough shit for a lifetime tonight?" her older self asked Utah.

The genius just smiled. She looked faded now, the actress noted, like weeds along a highway in September,

50

like the mountains when the leaves had lost their fire. She didn't have time to wonder at the change, however; her student self was speaking.

"…and I'll be doing Rich…Richard from *Richard III*."

The young woman tilted her right shoulder and angled her left foot onto the instep. The fingers of one hand curled as if she slept unsoundly. The woman she would be in eleven years could not help but feel a needle-prick of pride. The effect was subtle, graceful—all the things she admired most about her acting, when she had acted. When it had still seemed possible.

"Now is the winter of our discontent/ Made glorious summer by this sun of York."

Her voice, usually low and quiet when she was offstage, filled the studio to its dusty corners; one student who had fallen into a rock-like sleep opened her eyes and squirmed like an irritated cat.

Ebenezer raised her hands as if orating.

And all the clouds that lour'd upon our house
In the deep bosom of the ocean buried.
Grim-visaged war hath smooth'd his wrin-
    kled front;
  And now, instead of mounting barded
    steeds
 To fright the souls of fearful adversaries,
 He capers nimbly in a lady's chamber
 To the lascivious pleasing of a lute.

Her lips hitched into a sneer, and the last word came out sharp and vicious, a hornet's sting against a too-soft palm. Her fingers, tipped in black and glossed like a mirror's surface, twitched once…twice. Her voice grated like a saw across a rusted pipe as she turned to Lydia and paced forward one step. Two. Quiet—oh, so quiet, oh, so cold—and restrained. Her gray eyes could have been December.

> But I, that am not shaped for sportive tricks,
> Nor made to court an amorous looking-
>   glass;
> I, that am rudely stamp'd, and want love's
>   majesty
> To strut before a wanton ambling nymph;
> I, that am curtail'd of this fair proportion,
> Cheated of feature by dissembling nature,
> Deformed, unfinish'd, sent before my time
> Into this breathing world, scarce half made
>   up,
> And that so lamely and unfashionable
> That dogs bark at me as I halt by them;
> Why, I, in this weak piping time of peace,
> Have no delight to pass away the time,
> Unless to spy my shadow in the sun
> And descant on mine own deformity."

As each line shivered past her lips, the rusty whisper snarled into a shout that snapped off as if a door had opened, as if someone had overheard her past self's recitation and did not care for it. The younger Ebenezer lowered her eyes to her curled fingers and considered them.

> And therefore, since I cannot prove a lover,
> To entertain these fair well-spoken days,

I am determined to prove a villain
And hate the idle pleasures of these days.

"Plots have I laid," she said, at once attentive, her gaze focused once again upon the other students.

…Inductions dangerous,
By drunken prophecies, libels and dreams,
To set my brother Clarence and the king
In deadly hate the one against the other.
Dive, thoughts, down to my soul: here
Clarence comes.

She paused a bit too long before she dropped her pose, righting her body once again into the small slouch that persisted even after two sessions of Alexander Technique.

The applause were middling but not insincere. Most of her classmates still looked listless or sleepy.

Lydia's expression, however, was as unreadable as the older Ebenezer had always remembered it—somewhere between interested and unmoved.

"Thank you, Ebenezer. Your contemporary selection?"

"I've picked something from Sheila Callaghan's *Tumor*," the student said, her fingers barely fidgeting with the hem of her T-shirt.

"I wasn't half as good at that. Contemporary things, I mean. Theatre always felt older to me, like it was…" Her vision watered, and her voice trailed off. "Fuck," she whispered, lifting her wrist to scrub it away.

"Is something the matter?" the wizened genius inquired. Her lips were now the copper of an autumn sunset.

"What a stupid question." The wetness would not leave, so Ebenezer dug at it with her knuckles. Beneath her eyelids, her vision sparked. "I worked nonstop on that piece—I mean *nonstop*. Hard on the other one, too, but it didn't matter as much. Lydia was going to direct *Richard III* in February—nonstandard cast, she said. And it was perfect. I thought so, anyway."

Time must have shifted once again, she decided, because her younger self was now returning to her seat, both hands in the pocket of her blazer, where she knew they would be fiddling with a quarter.

"Thanks, Ebenezer. Good work. Bold choices," Lydia said, and her student blushed. "The second one was really fun. I think you really caught the spirit of Callaghan's work. But I think the first might have been a little too ambitious."

"Ambitious?" the student repeated.

Ebenezer flinched with her.

"Well, it's a very big role," her teacher explained. "A lot of actors who have been in the business a long time struggle with it—like Hamlet or Lear or, hell, Lady M, if you want an example that's usually played by women. It's hard, one of the hardest ones in English-language theatre, as far as I'm concerned, and not even they do it so good. I didn't think Ian McKellen did such a good job, for example."

Ebenezer nodded, looking more than a little bit downcast. The expressiveness of her face made her older self wince; it would be years yet before she perfected her frozen, unrevealing smile.

The sleepy student raised her hand. Lydia nodded. "Jill?"

"I think ambitious is a good word," the blond girl said—more than somewhat tartly, in Ebenezer's more adult opinion. "It's…I guess I didn't really understand what was going on here, you know? Whether you were talking to an audience or to *the* audience."

"I kind of saw it as kind of both." Ebenezer pressed her feet together. "In the movie you mentioned, Lydia, that's how they do it. I thought it was pretty effective."

"Yes, but a monologue should be an actor's own— well, as much as anything can be your own," Lydia said.

Another student raised her hand.

"Nanami? Your thoughts?"

Nanami flicked a lock of straight black hair from her eyes.

"I didn't really understand the pacing. I think your transitions could have been a lot clearer, Ebenezer."

"Well, what I was trying to go for was—"

Lydia raised her hand slowly, in the placating gesture she always used for freshmen and for actors on the verge of melting down.

"Remember, those directors at Playwrights Horizons won't be giving you a Q-and-A, either. If your intention doesn't come across for someone, then your performance didn't work for them."

"Oh." Ebenezer's face reddened down to her neck. "Sorry."

Her older self turned away from the scene as the critique continued.

"I've seen enough here," she told the genius.

"But I don't see why," Utah said as the room swirled into shadows at their backs. "You felt terrible, but they were hardly being abusive. And if an actress doesn't go to school to learn, then what were you doing there?"

Ebenezer's heart kicked at her ribs. Suddenly, she wondered what had become of that black blazer—her hands ached to hide inside it now.

"I didn't expect to be perfect, all right? It was just *different*. From anything I'd done before, in high school or even community theatre. I got direction, and suggestions, but nothing like twenty people all firing off different opinions at once while we couldn't even have a conversation. Maybe they were all used to it—half of them came from fine arts high schools where I guess this kind of thing was typical."

She shrugged. "It was all like *Alice in Wonderland* after I got that acceptance letter. I didn't know what was supposed to be typical for awhile. And when I figured it out, it was too late. I was just that girl who couldn't do her makeup right, and who sounded like she was from 'Texas or somewhere.' And it only got worse."

Her wrists felt so heavy she could have fallen to the floor.

"Well, I wasn't there," Utah said tentatively. "But I think that teacher liked you."

Ebenezer shook her head.

"No. Maybe a bit at first. But not really. See, I fucked that up, too."

She did not need to look behind her to know the scene had changed again, that the light had softened from the studio's too-harsh fluorescents to the edgeless glow of a desk lamp. The heaviness persisted, but Ebenezer turned as if her bones were magnetized.

Then, and now, Lydia's office reminded Ebenezer of standing inside a nugget of cut amber. The lights were always low and warm to help stave off all but the stealthiest of migraines. Two space heaters purred like soporific tabbies as the delft low-hanging winter evening peered through the window.

"Um... Ms. Bradstreet?"

The future Ebenezer's neck warmed again as Lydia looked up from her papers, her pallor filling up her eyes with shadows.

The student hesitated underneath the lintel.

"Is...Is now a bad time?"

"No, no. It's fine. Sorry." Lydia rubbed her forehead. "Just a little tired, that's all." Her smile was strained but gentle as ever. "Have a seat, Ebenezer. What can I do for you?"

"Well..." The teenager folded her fingers over the back of the wooden chair. "You said if we had any questions about auditions, that we could ask you?"

"Mhm." Lydia clasped her hands on the desktop. When she did not prompt further, Ebenezer stumbled on.

"Well, I was just wondering...what did I do wrong?"

It was the same thing she had asked after that dreadful class. The same thing she had asked each following week.

Lydia's voice thinned with her smile.

"It's not a question of wrong, Ebenezer. It's what a director *needs*." Her tone spoke the words she never would: *You know this. We've discussed this many times.*

"I know. You're right. I meant..." Ebenezer fumbled with her hoodie. "What can I improve on? Did I overact? Was it my projection?"

"I thought you understood—that monologue was too ambitious. Especially given the situation. This wasn't a callback, Ebenezer. You should have put together something else. If this had been an audition for anybody else, they would have seen your Richard as presumption, not eagerness."

"But if you'll just let me explain!"

The sigh would have been imperceptible to anyone who did not know Lydia.

"You've explained just fine, Ebenezer. But I'm not going to change my mind. And if you did *this* with any director? Word would get out, and you'd have a lot more problems than just one disappointment."

The student's hands flew up like sparrows trying to protect their nests.

"No! That's not what I mean. I'm not...I didn't come here to change your mind or say you were wrong. I'm sorry, I don't mean to press. I just..."

"I just want it so bad," her elder self murmured. "And I don't understand."

Lydia looked at her for a moment, grimacing in the tight, thin way that meant she was thinking of diplomacy.

"Okay," she said at last. "Okay. Apology accepted. I misunderstood. Long day and all. But, Ebenezer, look. You made it *here*, into a program that gets at least a thousand applications every year. You know how much that means? But that's only the first step. You've got to work with talent, just like you work your body in Alexander Technique, or your voice. And if you rush that, you get injured, right?"

"Yeah. I know."

Lydia's smile returned. "So, slow down, woman! You've got four years, and a lifetime after that. Watch some bad TV. Maybe go out to a party once in awhile— I know the others would really like to see you there."

Ebenezer stopped her shrug half-done to nod earnestly instead.

"The thing about chasing down perfection is that it's kind of like a Ponzi scheme—you invest and invest, but in the end you pay out much more than you get back."

"Then...I'm sorry, but what should I do, then? If I'm not working at being perfect."

Her teacher pointed to the side of her desk.

"Come here, kid. I can't get up to tell you." When Ebenezer complied, Lydia placed one heavy hand on her shoulder. "Let me tell you a little secret someone passed along to me at your age, back when I was just trying to get to callbacks. It's not about being the best. It's about being the best Lydia I can be, the best Ebenezer *you* can be. It's about being enough."

"Enough," Ebenezer repeated. She did not sound convinced.

Lydia patted her shoulder before releasing it.

"Just...try to remember that, okay? I don't want to see you get burned out here. That happens more often in this business than you'd think." Her hand returned to her forehead, which now appeared cratered and moist. "I'd like to continue this conversation, but I think I should probably go home now. Looks like the pills ain't gonna cut it today."

"Oh." The teenager swallowed. "Sorry. Can I...call a cab, maybe?"

Lydia waved her away as she eased up from her chair.

"I can make it that far. You go on to rehearsals. Remember, Brecht is a demanding master. Travis wouldn't have cast you in the ensemble if he didn't have faith in you, too."

"Okay. Thanks, Lydia. And…sorry if I made your headache worse."

"Hell," her professor laughed. "If I was that sensitive, I'd've retired already. See you tomorrow?"

"Yeah. Tomorrow."

But when her younger self smiled, it was all teeth, all sweetness. Entirely fake.

The room dissolved in a swirl of lavender and honey.

"She never cast me in a play, you know," Ebenezer said. "Not even as a guard. And when I asked her for a letter of recommendation—not for anything world-shattering, just for a summer scholarship—she said she couldn't recommend me in good conscience. Guess who graduated with the shittiest resumé in her class?"

"And everything depended upon that?"

Ebenezer swiped a hand through her tangled hair.

"That isn't the point. For someone who said she cared so much about us, she sure didn't lift a finger for anyone who really needed it."

"And did you?"

Ebenezer folded her arms and stared across the stage's empty, red-lit expanse.

"If you're asking me that, then why the hell are you here? I had no idea what to do there. Nothing but

60

try and try, and that just wasn't right. I guess the secret was just not to give a fuck.

"God, the look on her face all that time. She was so excited, so full of life and thinking that the world really, really gave a damn. She didn't look where she was going." She swallowed down the hotness in her throat. " I...I hate her. I betrayed her. If she knew what she'd become, she'd hate me, too, and I can't go back."

The snowflakes fell upon her eyelashes.

Scene VI

An Old Contract

"What?"

Ebenezer blinked and found the landscape had changed. She now looked out again upon the campus's snowy courtyard, the cold bench and the trees leaning all at angles as the city rumbled into evening. The snowflakes drifted slowly, as if they had no desire to join the dishwater-colored mess the city's exhaust pipes were steadily making of their family and friends.

She recognized her twenty-year-old form as it struggled through the wind between the monolithic buildings. Her hair was just as long and snarled then as now, and the black wool coat she'd bought to look sophisticated had accompanied her every winter after.

Somewhere a door must have opened, because another black coat was approaching.

Scrubbing away her icy tears, Ebenezer rounded on the genius, her knuckles and her eyes still raw.

"I don't want to see this. How many times do I have to say that?"

Utah did not answer.

"I told you, I don't want to see this!"

The deserted courtyard stared back at her.

"Utah?"

Someone's lost chemistry notes fluttered wetly past like wings.

"*Utah?*"

The chill along her arms did not come from that long-ago winter. Ebenezer's breath clouded her vision as she searched for her companion behind tree and trash bin, under bench or inside door—no hint of sage or sandstone. With a great defeated sigh, she slumped onto the base of a tall statue.

"Be careful. That's my toe."

The Genius of Utah had taken on a skin like weathered granite, and her nipples stood out hard as steel ingots. Despite the clinging damp, her thorny hair now hung limp and dry as autumn grass.

"Utah? What's the matter? You don't look so well."

"I'm a little beyond my bounds, don't you think?" The genius gestured at the snow-strewn courtyard and the two approaching women. Ebenezer did not listen for an answer.

Marley was running to her younger self, her green scarf flying back and up like a sail. Everything else about her was red—her cheeks so bright Ebenezer could see the capillaries. Her waist-length hair was like a wound against the sky.

"Ebenezer? Ebenezer! Wait!"

The student turned slowly, as if stepping from a reverie.

"Don't wait!" Her older self hissed. "Go catch the Six-train!"

63

But she stood there still as sleep, her black coat flapping around her ankles.

It was all happening again.

"It *is* Ebenezer, right?" The younger Marley rubbed her mittened hands together, a tic she favored well into her twenties. Then, as now, Ebenezer found it utterly adorable.

"Right. Sorry, but I don't..."

"Marley. Marley James. It's okay, I just transferred here, and we just have that modern drama class together. I sit way in the back."

Ebenezer nodded.

"And we both tried out for *Suddenly Last Summer*. Um. You were really great as Nellie, but I thought you deserved Alma. Your audition was way better."

"Thanks."

The sharp wind blew between them. The current Ebenezer felt her stomach heat and knew her younger self felt exactly the same.

"You know damned well who she is, Marley," she muttered.

Marley worked the toe of her boot into the grungy snow and found her voice before the wind could speak for her again.

"So, you know how we have to do that presentation on Noh theatre? I wanted to do *Lady Aoi*, and since we're supposed to work in pairs and Dr. Schaeffer said we could pick—"

"Sure. I'd like to."

Marley blinked, and then her full lips pulled into a smile.

"Really? Um. That's great! Hey, um, if you're just going home now...maybe we could talk about it? Like at coffee…or hot chocolate, since I know Mormons don't drink that."

Student Ebenezer's head snapped back with the force of her laugh. The redness in her cheeks had nothing at all to do with the weather.

"I'm sorry. I thought—it's coffee, right? And most hot drinks? I'm sorry. I didn't mean to…"

Ebenezer coughed her snickering down.

"No, you didn't. Trust me. I'm not a Mormon, much to everyone's disappointment. And hot chocolate's nice."

"Well. Great! I know this place over on Christopher that does twenty different kinds. But, you've been here since last year, so you probably know all about that."

The pad of her mitten enfolded Ebenezer's knuckles quite before either noticed what was happening.

"I think we'd be great for each other," she said.

And they both knew what that meant.

"So, if it's okay to ask?" Marley said as they walked away together. "It's…Usually Ebenezer's a man's name. So…"

Ebenezer chuckled. "I'm not a Mormon, but I *am* from Utah. Where, when you get a girl baby, you think, 'You know what this kid needs? Let's name her after her great-grandfather! That won't give her any self-esteem problems, ever!'"

Marley laughed into a mittened hand.

"So, how about Marley? That's kind of…"

"Oh. Don't know there. I think my mother had a friend or something. Thought it was pretty. 'It sounds like marble,' she once told me. How's that for weird, huh?"

They smiled as they moved off through the snow.

Chilly Utah stood behind her, tall and gray as any New York building as the students exited the courtyard, Marley bouncing as she waved her unused hand in full-blown conversation, Ebenezer walking stiff and stately but with a purpose her older self mourned.

"That's a rare sight, you smiling."

"It's hard not to smile at Marley,"

Ebenezer watched her past recede into the snow-swirled gray of memory and distance until it turned a corner and lost itself. The winter felt much colder, and she felt decidedly thirty.

"I didn't date back in Vernal or even Salt Lake, not that you don't know. It was always just schoolwork, or trying out for some theatre camp or other, or working at the flower shop to get money for them. And none of the girls saw me like that—the way they went on about prom and marriage, anyway.

"Not that it mattered. I was just too busy. And then, when I came here, suddenly I had Christopher Street, and Pride Parades and Marley to show me…well, just how lonely I was. How lonely I…" Ebenezer hugged herself. In their garlands of fog, the buildings suddenly felt too big.

She was so very tired. So very heavy. Every limb felt as though it had been chained down to concrete. Chained…

"I don't want to think about it anymore. Take me back to my apartment. It's ugly and it's empty and it sucks, but it's home. It has to be."

Overhead, the light shifted suddenly from chill to red, and the spotlight hummed back on. The genius had returned to her umber self.

"This is where I leave you."

Ebenezer wondered if one could feel concurrently regretful and relieved.

"Do you remember the last time you visited the Vernal desert?" Utah asked, as if she had again heard her charge's thoughts. Most likely she could, Ebenezer decided.

"I went out in May, the day before my flight. The Colorado River was still fat from winter, and sometimes I thought it was trying to speak. I took my sandals off and just…dug my toes into the sand. To feel the heat.

"The rabbit brush was trying to get up courage to bloom, and I could see all the way up to Split Mountain. It looked like some big cloud that came down to earth when the planet was still bubbling and decided to stay. The sky was so clear that day. Not a single cloud." Her eyes stung, but she blinked the feeling away. "How come I don't get to see *that* memory?"

"Some memories are close enough you don't have to," the genius said. She laid her large hand on Ebenezer's head. It felt like clear desert sunlight, like the red sand hot between her toes, like its own great heart. "My hand is always on your head, Ebenezer. Always on your head."

With a lizard's wink of a smile, she vanished, and the lights came down like a fist.

Act III

The Second of the
Three Spirits

Scene I

A Jolly Giant

Heat on her brow—her palm. Ebenezer dozily cracked one eye and wriggled the fingers spider-spread through her hair. The elbow she had used as a pillow pulsed and stung as she raised her head, and then her body.

The streetlights covered the floor with honey, and the thick snowflakes moth-fluttering past her window gave the living room a dreamy feel, but it was unmistakably her apartment. She blinked to verify—no stage or sand was in sight.

Always on your head.

"Strange dream," she murmured. "Strange."

Feeling particularly cold, she fetched her tattered bathrobe from its hook then, thinking better, her coat from its slump upon the sole remaining chair. Thick wool socks and galoshes followed—both Marley's mismatched cast-offs. Still cold, Ebenezer switched on the kitchenette's fluorescents and put on the teakettle, thankful not to see red and fallow sand veining her walls again.

"*Really* strange dream." Stranger for its gradually diminishing strangeness—save for the rock-woman, it was nothing but a crawl of memories.

But *what* memories.

The kettle's melancholy whistle startled her. Shutting off the burner, she fixed peppermint tea in her favorite mug and returned to her makeshift bed. She thought of reaching for the TV's power button, but the clock read one a.m., and the static beyond the windows was far more interesting. She stared at it and sipped, thinking static thoughts punctuated every now and then by the smell of sage.

A strange dream and nothing more, and anyway, it did not matter. What good were memories if they only told stories you already knew and couldn't change?

The radiator whispered *gone, gone, gone*; near the bottom of her cup, Ebenezer realized it had *truly* gone. Shivering, she padded over to give it a thorough examination. The pipes were barely lukewarm under their scabrous white paint.

In her peripheral vision, something fluttered across the window glass like the shadow of a great wing. The skin on her back constricted, and she turned so fast she nearly dropped her mug. Outside her, beneath her, she found only snow, but snow that fell in great bird feathers. Moving closer, she hoped to see something in the street—a taxi cab, a caterpillar of a bus, even a drug dealer's van with its inconspicuous lights.

She stared until the clock blinked 1:15; not even a pedestrian burdened with overdue parcels straggled past. The snow was inches deep and unmarred even by a stray cat's paw print.

Ebenezer forced the shiver to recede into her lower spine.

"It's just coincidence. It's cold, it's Christmas Eve and, hell, it's practically a blizzard out there!" Still, it was New York, the city sleep has never visited, and goose pimples pricked her arms unbidden.

Suddenly, Ebenezer was angry.

"This is bullshit. I'm going to go downstairs and look outside, and there will be taxis, and lit bodegas, and drunks braying in the doorways, just like always." Once again, her palm cupped her forehead. "And I'm talking to myself. Again."

Nobody heard, of course, but the embarrassment still stung.

She wound her scarf around her neck and locked her door. The angled staircase was dizzying to navigate, even on her rare clear-headed days.

Outside, the night was every bit as cold as it had appeared, and every bit as empty. The street lamps still nestled all alone in their amber triangles, and the imprints of Ebenezer's boots on the stoop seemed the only ones for miles.

It had to be coincidence. It had to be. She repeated the assertion, sometimes silently and sometimes aloud, as she tracked down the sidewalks then the unplowed streets as if to tempt the traffic to return and bury her. The next street was no livelier, nor the next. Two avenues gave her only darkness, snow and wind, which howled more with every step.

She had just passed the fashionable brownstones of 103rd Street when she heard it, soft yet distinct beneath the blustering—a steady, glassy crunch.

Someone was following.

Ebenezer froze mid-step and felt her blood run cold. Eleven years of her mother's paranoia chased through her mind at once: *Don't go out after dark. Don't go any-*

where alone. Get a taser—hell, get two! She had dismissed her near-hysteria over Kitty Genovese with a lot of cursing and a summary of fifty years of feminism. Now, here in these ghost-town streets, it all felt like so many words.

The footsteps had stopped. As the wind swirled through her hair like fingers, she took a calming breath and waited for a lull to speak.

"Hey, motherfucker. I've kicked asses bigger and tougher than yours, and if you spend Christmas Day in the ER that suits me just fine."

Regretting that she had always been far more interested in Alexander and Pilates than in self-defense, Ebenezer turned slowly, her eyes wide. The street was all dark air and snow.

And then the sound like crunching mirrors came at her from the left, at a full-out run.

She pivoted and swung her fist, connected with a shadow.

"Sorry," said a woman's voice behind her. "Didn't mean to scare you. It's so fuckin' bad out here tonight even I can barely see."

Ebenezer had a feeling the world had torn open once again.

"Who are you?" she said carefully.

This time when the world lit up, the street became the stage, its players Ebenezer and an electric woman. She took up no more than the dimensions of one townhouse, yet she contained a skyline. Her body was a collage of advertisement, stock-exchange and news tickers, but where headlines, numbers, and soda bottles should have flown past like arterial blood, a thousand images—a million—cycled.

The corner of 71st and Amsterdam...

The heart of an Asian grocery's sunflower...

A homeless woman dozing lightly in a Battery Park bush, and the policeman who told her to move on...

The Chrysler's needle in foul weather...

A scaffolding's lonely orange canopy...

Her head blazed with a crown of neon light. She was...

Like staring at all the city all at once.

Ebenezer felt herself pitch sideways, and then the sting of snow upon her cheek. A steely hand jostled her shoulder.

"Kid? Hey, kid. You all right?"

"Ngh." Ebenezer confirmed, staying where she'd landed.

"Here, I'll tone it down." The neon light filtering through her eyelids diminished substantially. "Is this better? C'mon, kid. I won't hurt you any more than looking at Times Square."

Shielding her eyes, although she knew it would do no good, Ebenezer looked up again and found a diminished version of the colossus. A mere hundred tickers clothed her neon body, which suddenly sprouted a subway train that roared across the harsh plane of her belly before tunneling into her naval.

"Who are you?" she asked a little louder, though she already knew the answer.

The neon woman rolled her yellow eyes.

"You've lived in me eleven years, and you can't figure it out?"

"You're New York City."

The city inclined her towering head.

"The Genius of the Five Boroughs, its Eight Winds, and Twenty Million Stories. But just New York is okay." She observed Ebenezer quietly for several moments as the snow howled down around her. "You came looking for me."

"Not exactly," Ebenezer got back up and brushed the snow from her coat. "Where is everybody?"

A smile flashed across the genius's face.

"You think *everybody* wants to be out in this shit?"

"Somebody's always out. You should know that."

"Yeah, and those people can find better things to do somewhere else than the Upper West Side if I want. You should know that, too. Anyway, that's not what's happening."

When Ebenezer just stared at her, the genius sighed.

"You're not on One-hundred-third street," she explained, sounding very tired. "This is the One-hundred-third of your own, private New York—permafrost the whole year and population one." She indicated Ebenezer with a finger like a steel crossbeam. "You live there every day. You walk down its streets and smell its sewers and stare into its shop windows. Doesn't matter that there's people on all sides—they're just shadows as far as *you* can see them. So, why are you so surprised to come here literally?

"Hey, cheer up," she said as Ebenezer frowned and crossed her arms. "Nearly twenty million people here, and every one's a lonely bastard. Even the socialites come here sometimes."

"I disagree."

The genius shrugged shoulders upon which two museums perched.

"If it lives in a body, it can be lonely. Want to see?"

"Not really." Ebenezer shoved her hands deep into her pockets. "And I agree—it's much too cold for anyone. I'm going back to bed."

She had gone three steps into the snowstorm when the genius spoke again.

"Well, all right. But I'll take you to see Marley."

Ebenezer hated being manipulated; a job with quotas and vague threats from supervisors was more than enough to tolerate each day. She did not, however, let that conceal her excitement.

"Marley?"

New York City laughed, a subway rumble and bushorn blast.

"Yep. Thought that'd get you."

She turned and started walking, leaving Ebenezer scrambling to follow her through the cotton-fall of snow.

"You'd better not be fucking with me," she grumbled.

"Lady, I fuck with people every day. But I don't lie—I'm exactly what I am. Come on, already. I don't got all night."

Ebenezer sped up until their strides matched.

"You don't need to be so rude."

Another laugh. "Eleven years here, and you still think that about me? Sexy."

Ebenezer grunted. Just as on the subways and the buses, silence, she decided, made for the best conversation.

The genius led her eastward, past Amsterdam and all the way to Columbus Avenue. Within one block, the streets became as populous as (Ebenezer glanced at a shuttered bank's digital clock—two a.m.) on any other night. Couples of all combinations huddled close as conspiracies, laughing as they shivered. The neon greens and purples of restaurant signs patched the snow. Two homeless men sat on the steps of a church clutching coffee cups, their hands and faces a shocked kind of wrinkled tan. Taxis and trucks scuttled past, plentiful as roaches.

At first, Ebenezer thought nothing of the night wanderers who passed them, text-messaging and mumbling of selfishness and plagues. On most days, the city had no time for her, and she was just as happy to return the favor. But when one man shoved her into a wall on his way to flag a taxi, her appreciation of benign neglect ended.

"Fucking assbag!" she shouted at his back.

He climbed into the cab without so much as a flipped bird. *Typical.*

"Oh. Yeah. When you're with me, people are liable to not see you."

Ebenezer flexed her aching fingers.

"Excuse me?"

"You ever look up at the skyscrapers? The subway stations? And go 'Wow, I'm in New York!'?"

"I'm not exactly a tourist, as you keep pointing out."

"Right. You don't notice; you're too busy living *her*. Ebenezer, I give you the reason why I can walk down any street and no one says, 'Oh God! There's a fifty-foot building shaped like a woman!' Of course, that goes for anyone walking with me."

"So I get the bruises but not the recognition. Awesome." But she was careful to follow closer. Soon, they

78

stopped before another row of townhouses where snow settled pleasantly upon stoops and pike-like iron gates.

"So, Marley moved close to Central Park?" Her teeth clenched. "Nice."

And just like Marley, too. When had there ever been a situation that didn't turn out in her favor? She touched shit, Ebenezer had often remarked, and it turned to gold, while everything *she* touched turned into shit.

Naturally, Marley hadn't liked that one bit; but lucky, special people never liked hearing how special and lucky they were, Ebenezer had always quipped. And things had gone to hell inevitably after that.

"So, are you going in, or is getting snowed on just that cool?"

Ebenezer's eyes snapped back into focus.

"What?"

"Now who's rude? I was just saying that we're not here to see Marley."

"Then what the fuck—"

The genius held up one flashing hand.

"Chill. I said I'd take you to her; I didn't say when. Hey, I'm New York, hon. You gotta be specific with me."

Ebenezer rolled her eyes.

"Look—fine, whatever. Who the hell lives here, and why should I give a fuck?"

"Seeing that he goes out of his way to be nice to your skinny ass, the least you can do is pay Fred Carter a visit."

"He's my supervisor. Some guy at work. It isn't like he'd care. You just don't *do* that."

"Like you know what people actually do." the genius said as she climbed the steps. Ebenezer wondered when she'd shrunk down to human dimensions. Perhaps that was just one more perk of being a city—the ability to be any size.

"You've got that right. What?" The city blinked as Ebenezer stared at her. "Relax, kid. I don't make a habit of reading minds. It's creepy, and besides? Why bother when your face does all the work for me."

"Actors are supposed to be expressive. And I *do* know how people work."

"So *that's* why you've got such a shiny disposition."

"You're really starting to piss me off." But Ebenezer followed her through the door anyway.

"Wah-wah." The genius fluttered her electric fingers. "So I'm blunter than sweet little Utah. Deal with it."

"Well, I wish you'd go away, and she'd come back!"

"Can't do that, little one. Your present's not exactly her jurisdiction, and neither are my streets. You saw how wilted she got when she tried. And unlike her, I don't give a damn if you're bored or uncomfortable. So shut your hole if you want to see Marley."

"Bitch," Ebenezer muttered as they took the ornate stairs.

"No, sweetie. You're *my* bitch tonight."

Ebenezer closed and opened her mouth several times like a caught fish, but not finding a retort that felt quite vicious enough, she kept her thoughts to herself. She barely had the time to craft one anyway—on the second floor, New York City stopped in front of an oak-stained door emblazoned with a filigreed 202.

"Huh. Who would've thought Fred had such a good place." She butted a boot-tip against the plush red carpet.

"Yeah, who'd've thought that people had lives out-side of when you see them?"

Ebenezer aimed a kick at the genius's circuited an-kle as she passed, ghost-like, through the wood. Her toe collided with the paneling instead.

The genius's head emerged.

"Oh, by the way? You should always hold my hand whenever we're going somewhere locked. Since I'm everywhere anyway, I can get away with it. But you…?"

"Fine, just shut up."

Ebenezer grabbed the offered hand; it felt like how she had always imagined the screen of a flashing road sign felt—warm and bumpy, but in some places smooth as neon tubing.

The genius gave a tug, and she found herself in Fred's kitchen.

Scene II

Yes and No

It was much cleaner than her own, and far more spacious. Two Ebenezers could have lain toe-to-toe on the neat cream tiles with arms stretched to aching limits, and enough space would have remain for Fred's cat to tiptoe by. At least, she assumed the tabby drinking from the metal bowl was his and not some visiting friend's.

As a large man lumbered past, the creature's eyes dilated, and she bolted for the table's overhang. He was built like Fred, and as he eased himself down into an easy chair, Ebenezer noted he shared her supervisor's broad forehead and puffy cheeks.

Brothers?

Fred looked up from the sofa where he was doodling—somewhat obviously, in her opinion—on the pages of a sudoku book.

"Everything all right there, Carl?"

"Yeah, yeah, it's good. Just thought I heard someone banging on the door."

"It's probably those kids across the hall."

Fred put the book aside and reached for a bowl of Doritos perched on a nearby cushion.

82

"Their parents ever heard of bedtimes?"

"Heck, Carl, it's Christmas Eve. You remember how hard Grandma fought to get us settled down?"

"Yeah, but we didn't go kicking the neighbors' doors till Santa came. She'd'a beat that shit right out of us."

"I know. I talked to Gladys back when they kept knocking and hiding. They're good kids, really, and just acting out because their daddy's gone."

"Beat till we couldn't sit for days," Carl grunted. "Now, don't you eat all them chips, Fred. I ain't going out after dark for more."

"I keep telling you, New York's no more dangerous than Louisville. Probably a whole lot less."

"And you ain't been there since your folks moved out to the whitest little city in the country!"

"Hey, I get that it makes you nervous, but if you're gonna find work here, you've got to go *out* sometime. But, man, if you wanna go back, I understand." He passed the bowl to his…cousin? Friend? Ebenezer still could not decide.

Carl took it and dug his hand into the chips.

"Yeah, back to that empty house, and all Delores's friends telling me I didn't do right by that woman." He spread the handful of cool ranch chips out on a plate.

"You tried your best, Carl. Sometimes these things just don't work out."

It was a platitude, and judging by his too-wide smile, Ebenezer guessed Fred knew that.

"You can be really shitty at this comfort business, you know that?" But Carl seemed to be trying for a grin.

"Yeah, I know. I'm just really sorry, and there's no good way to say that."

83

"Hell, it don't matter. The kids say it's never too late to start your life again." Carl munched on a chip, looking thoughtful. "How about you get me a job down at that call center where you work? I hear those places are always looking, and I done my share of telemarketing."

It seemed to Ebenezer the air had been sucked right out of the room. Fred's face twitched, as if he was fighting to keep his chips down..

"Trust me, man. You do *not* want to work for Carker and Tulkinghorn."

"And why not? Man's gotta eat, and it's not right to mooch off you at my age."

"They will pick you dry."

Carl just laughed. "Man, I worked repossessions! This ain't no different."

"They will pick you dry," Fred repeated in a tone that shocked Ebenezer with its edge. "You *think* it's no different from a crappy college job or a high school job selling…I don't know, satellite or magazine subscriptions. That you'll be there just till something better.

"But something better never comes because nobody's hiring historians. And when your numbers aren't up because you just can't yell at those people to pay up any longer, they tell you that's it. Get them up, or else it's your ass."

He wiped his hand down his face, flicking off a sheen of sweat.

"So you figure, yeah, it's you or them, and you yell at those people. You threaten them with laws that don't exist and say words your bishop probably doesn't even know exist. Pretty soon, your numbers come up, and they give you a promotion—though never quite where the white kids are, even when you don't have to do the phones anymore."

He paused, as if anticipating an interjection from Carl. When none came, he shook his head.

"Kids go in there thinking it'll be easy. One week later, they leave crying. And the ones that stay …" He rubbed his forehead again. "There's this Utah girl, Ebenezer."

"Is this that I'm One Are You, Too? business?"

Fred rolled his eyes. "Not everyone's a Mormon back there. She doesn't strike me as the religious type, either, and I don't really think she does the friend thing. She came over three years ago, about this time of year, if I remember. Acted all interested in the interviews, said she'd lost her telemarketing job when it went over to Pakistan. But what she just really wanted was to act.

"You can tell the type—they say they're into it, but they just look sad or bored, like they'd rather be somewhere else. But she was friendly enough. Then one day, she came in and…" He turned his palms up— *poof!* "It was like something died. Now she just gives me this thousand-watt stage smile." He closed his eyes. "I worry about her."

"And why's this girl your business?"

Fred sucked a breath in through his teeth. For the first time, Ebenezer realized they were straight as fence posts, as gravestones.

"It's the same smile *I've* put on for five years."

In the pause that followed, the tabby leaped onto his lap with a shadow's grace. Fred stroked her arched

85

back gently as he stared forward, forward, as if he saw his own death lurking in the snow outside the window.

"They'll pick you dry," he repeated.

Neither man spoke for several minutes. At last, Carl hefted himself from the leather chair with a smoker's grunt. He stepped into Fred's line of vision until the supervisor looked right at him.

"Fred…look. I don't know what to tell you. It's not right. Me and Delores. You. Nothing's been right anywhere for a real long time. But, hell, it's Christmas Eve. I think we can let all that be for awhile. We got that nice take-out in the fridge, and you haven't even opened your mama's cookies. And I got that Bud—"

"You know I don't drink."

"Your bishop is not going to bust down the door and ground you!"

"I'll just have some Sprite."

Carl shrugged and lumbered over to the kitchen.

"You want the chow mein or the lo mein? Never could keep those straight."

Ebenezer didn't catch Fred's answer. The spirit's glass fingers closed around her wrist and tugged her back through the door as Carl peered into the fridge's amber light, his face worried, too, beneath its smile.

The plush hallway felt much colder and emptier than before. New York City had taken on the townhouse's colors—carmine-flushed and mahogany-haired. If she said anything smart, Ebenezer didn't notice as she brushed her fingers against the door. Through the wood she heard the pop of bottle caps—one…two.

"I didn't know." Her fingers traced a ring.

"What, you thought he was just happy all the time?"

"Shut up!" Ebenezer reddened all the same "But, yeah…I guess I just…didn't think of him like that. About his family, or how he smiles, or…a history degree?" She chuckled, but not meanly. Somehow, it suited him. "He's just Fred from work." Suddenly, she felt very cold and tired. "Can I see Marley now?"

The genius tossed her hair and descended the polished staircase like a flood.

"Guess again," she called over one Persian-patterned shoulder.

Ebenezer pelted after her, her knees complaining underneath her wool skirt the whole way down.

"You promised!" she accused. "You promised."

"Uh-huh. And remember what I said about eventuals?"

New York City took her through the front door; a wheeze of snow caught in the steely cables of her hair and dimmed the berry-like lights of her coronet. The abrupt change made Ebenezer's stomach pitch and her shoulders clench—why geniuses had to alter their appearance every ten seconds, she didn't know, but it was giving her a headache.

"Because life doesn't stand still." New York City winked one train-light eye. "And me least of all."

"Well, all *this* change is making me sick," Ebenezer snapped as the wind blasted down the street.

The eye had not moved from her.

"Maybe that's your problem." Then the genius was off again before her charge could dig up a retort. "Come on! We're going out to Brooklyn!"

Scene II

Chained Phantoms

The great bridge hung over the chilly Hudson like the backbone of some steel Pleistocene sea dweller. Ebenezer had crossed it only twice on foot—inexcusable, Bell insisted, for an immigrant of eleven years. But then, Bell was only twenty-two and had all the wit of a poached fish, so Ebenezer tended not to listen to her.

The snow beat around her head like moths, and the water beneath the metal arch sludged blackly between great whale backs of ice. The effect was as eerie as it was isolating, and as she passed over the roaring silence, Ebenezer was not surprised to find it full of ghosts.

They swirled through the night air and troubled the waves of darkness by the thousands. The sight alone was not exactly alarming—after this night's adventures, little in the way of spirits could have shocked her. But these were unlike any she had seen or even imagined.

All ages, all races, all sexes, each was weighted with frightening equipage, hung with chains from which parcels, furniture, microscopes, computers, and other sundries dangled like macabre charms on a sterling bracelet. Some lengths were short as a choker, others cocooned their bearers. Some howled through the air, their fetters dangling fifty feet from their wrists or ankles. For reasons she could not explain, Ebenezer found the last of these most terrifying.

She shrank back hard against New York City's electric warmth. Her wrists ached as if they were being pulled toward the ground by great magnets.

"What are they?" she whispered

"Specters. Memories. Regrets. A few whatevers." The genius leviathan's voice was surprisingly gentle and low, hardly louder than the deep water's heartbeat. "Mostly, they're the things you people leave behind."

"When we die?" Ebenezer stared at one hobbled woman dragging a chain studded with playbills and theatre masks.

"Yeah, sometimes. But it isn't what you think. Sometimes you can do that and still have a pulse."

Ebenezer was about to turn and ask how that was possible when two figures resolved from the mist. The first was a small woman huddled in a long black coat, her long hair a wreathe of tangles. The second was taller, paler, her hair like a wound against the sky.

Marley.

"She's just a memory," New York City shouted, but Ebenezer was already far away, her stick legs flailing, her twig arms reaching—Marley!

The mist sucked her into an afternoon of cold steel and tempera light.

Scene III

Contented with the Time

"How deep do you think it goes?" said the woman standing at Marley's side.

Ebenezer recognized herself at…twenty? Twenty-one? Anyway, she wore a hideous periwinkle hat with loose stitching—her mother had knitted it after her last hospital stay, but Ebenezer could not recall the year. Still, her face had that look of distant desperation she had come to associate with her early twenties.

Marley must have seen it, too, because she covered her girlfriend's ungloved knuckles with her hand.

"What are you thinking?"

Younger Ebenezer's mouth had pulled into a sour line. She stared at the waves left by a motorboat.

"Just what I said—how deep do you think the water goes?"

"Are you asking because of aesthetics, or out of scientific curiosity?"

Ebenezer directed the sour look at her. "

"Ah. Okay. Right. You're in a mood."

"You *know* why I'm asking," Ebenezer said in that sharp, impatient way her older self had honed to a needle's point.

"Sweetie…" Marley's hand slid into her hair. "It's just one audition. Just one role."

Ebenezer pulled away and slumped against the railing. That was how she did it in those days, her older self recalled. Now, she hid her need and disappointment behind a silence just as glacial as the clogged river whose depths she now searched.

But back then, she was all heat, all lava. She could see the explosion building capillary by capillary in her younger self's gray eyes. Vaguely, she wondered why Marley had liked her outbursts better than her quiet.

"Ebbie, please. You're not going to storm Broadway in a month!"

The backdraft flared.

"Like you just didn't, you mean."

"It's only swing and chorus every Thursday," Marley said meekly. "And besides, you have the Haverly. They love you there. They called you back, even!"

"It's off-off-Broadway. And let me give you some advice, because you're so very young—when you have something somebody doesn't have, don't ever use the word *just*."

"Ebbie…" Marley's hands were raised, as if her girlfriend's rage could take concrete form any minute. "Okay, okay, I'm really sorry. I just hate it when you're sad."

"Sometimes life *is* sad," Ebenezer huffed, returning to her slouch. She stared back into the water and spat over the side, but the fire had retreated.

Marley's gaze followed the globule down.

"Well, that's attractive," she said with a cheerfulness that had yet to be forced, or even strained.

Ebenezer grunted.

"Hey, I know it sucks. But it's Christmas. Almost."

Another grunt.

"Shall we look at reasons to be thankful? There's that box-office job you've got where they actually support actors' schedules. The Celexa isn't making your mom barf. And there's our real-adult apartment! And the Haverly, remember? In that awesome new play by that person you went to school with?"

"That person hated me. And if I can't act in something that will go anywhere, what good is any of that? I could have stayed in Salt Lake for all that. And still helped Mom."

"And had a hot girlfriend, too? Well, thanks. That makes me feel just great." But there was no edge to her voice as Marley hugged her arm. "Ebbie, New York City's got a million theaters. Not all of them can be stupid. And I mean, it's only some *Hello, Dolly!* revival. It's no guarantee I'll have work after. Or that you won't. Please, don't be jealous." She kissed her cheek. "It gives you wrinkles."

"I'm not jealous."

"Well, then don't be sad! And don't talk about jumping off, either. It just makes you sound like a Tennessee Williams heroine." She frowned. "And his later plays are boring and weepy. Don't be boring. Or weepy."

This coaxed out a smile.

"Yeah. Thanks, Marl. Sorry. It's just been a shitty week."

Marley kissed her cheeks, and then her forehead. "Then let's unshittify it. There's that new show over at the Looking Glass. All-female *Measure for Measure*."

"Like that will work."

Ebenezer shook her head as if to clear it of phantoms. She stepped back from the railing and twined her hand with Marley's.

"After, maybe we can go to Chinatown and get some of those dough balls you like."

Ebenezer massaged her forehead, her mood clearly improving.

"Yeah, if we wait until February. They only have those during lunar new year, I think."

"Well, uh…okay. That fish jerky stuff, then."

"Silly." Ebenezer leaned in for a kiss.

"Yeah, you like me silly."

The older Ebenezer flinched away before their lips could meet. When she looked back, both girls were gray and thin as the rest of the spirits misting on the air. Their echoes swirled beside the rail, conjoined, resolved into the heavy figure of a man. He hunched forward as Ebenezer's memory had, staring down into the three a.m. darkness.

Scene IV

Lamentation and Regret

How deep does it go, I wonder? Ebenezer could have sworn she heard him think.

It was then she noticed that the spirits, echoes, and other entities had taken an interest. One-by-one and two-by-three they converged on him like tailings to a magnet.

Some, their gaunt faces wide with terror, reached for him only to grab air. Others slung their rattling chains for his throat and waist, or leaped from the bridge to hover in the air before his face, which great tear lines had fractured like a continent. Their mouths moved slowly, but no sound issued save a whisper like the shift of heat over subway grate or static on a radio.

As Ebenezer strained closer to hear, an unseen hand somewhere twisted a dial and the rustling cleared into a chorus.

What's the point of living when you only fail?
No one will miss me. My family won't care.
I just want the pain to stop.

I can't do anything right.
Why won't it end?
I want to die.
Die.
Die.
Die.
Don't do it.

Ebenezer couldn't tell if she had thought the last words or spoken them aloud. The numbness creeping through her body now was as familiar as these violent commands. It felt like what she had always imagined one of Aunt Vona's jointless frozen Charlotte dolls experienced as she stood in her shadowbox nook, or perhaps what sinking through quicksand would be like. Her knees groaned, her shoulders pinched, and she felt dizzy.

She wondered how deep the river went.

"You would think..." The genius shook her head, her voice the angry growl of an emerging subway train. "...that death or distancing would make people a little more goddamned compassionate."

For the first time that evening, Ebenezer felt New York City's hand on her shoulder, firm and warm and gentle as the first glimpse of spring. As she shivered, the genius drew her mantel close around her body/them.

"Come on. I'll handle this," and her mighty arm hefted its steel torch high.

A sound like cab horns, drunkenness, flute calls and twenty million feet broke the night down the middle as the genius swung the torch like a wand; the warning lights upon her crown glowed red and green. It was the music of the city, Ebenezer realized as the phantoms took to shrieking flight.

Some, perhaps half, lingered in concern as the man stepped away from the edge, sank to his knees and wept into the concrete.

Huddled in the gentle hum of New York City's cloak, Ebenezer had no choice but to follow as the genius advanced and shook her torch like a censer over the prostrate figure. A familiar smell like sweat, grass, and sun on pavement wafted from its electric flames. Ebenezer had no name for it but excitement. It revived her, too.

After a few minutes spent in dutiful shaking, her yellow eyes half-lidded in what surprised Ebenezer as concern, the genius of the city lowered her torch back to her side. Its blaze snapped off, leaving ghostly orbs and streaks of light in Ebenezer's vision. When she blinked them off at last, she found the bridge as bare of supernatural activity as when they had approached.

Meanwhile, the genius was caressing the fallen man's hair. In response, he gave a half-hearted moan and shrank into a go-away-please curl.

"All right, looks like he's too fucked up to make it home," the city observed, as if she were only noting a change in weather.

Ebenezer found it difficult to speak. She finally managed a quiet, "What the hell just happened?"

The genius rolled her train-light eyes as she gathered the man into her arms.

"I give you the Brooklyn Bridge, Ebenezer: popular destination for the suicidally depressed since—oh, you know."

96

"Yeah, but what just *happened*?" she persisted, gesturing impotently from the broken man to the empty leap beyond the rail.

"The usual bitchery of life, now, then, forever, amen. And it's called compassion, Ebenezer. Something you might wanna learn sometime."

"Bullshit," Ebenezer spat, now feeling quite like herself again. "You don't show anybody mercy."

"Says you."

"Everyone knows that."

"*Everyone* knows that," the genius hurled back, stamping her great foot in childish petulance. "Says you, who hasn't looked for it in years."

Ebenezer felt her cheeks burn, and her gratitude for New York's protection evaporated as fast as the spirits had.

"What? After your mom slashes her wrists in front of you, suicide attempts kind of stop being anything but routine. I'm plenty compassionate!"

"Which is why you bully people for a living, right?"

"*Telling people to pay their debts isn't bullying!*"

"Again, could you speak louder? Someone on Staten Island's still asleep."

"Look, Fred was right. It's a shitty job, and nobody likes doing it—well, maybe Trent and Cynthia, but they've got problems, and most of us think they're sharks who somehow constructed human suits." The joke felt hollow even as she thought it. "Anyway, we can't just let people buy shit and never pay. That's how you end up where we are now. And I manage to pay my bills. Why can't they?"

It was a script she recited every day with the passion of a prayer she could not trust, and they both knew it.

New York City waved her steel hand wide, cutting off any more conversation (and when had she taken on a metallic sheen? Ebenezer wondered.)

"Well, you just keep chasing that rainbow. Meanwhile, this guy's not going to make it home all by himself."

Had the bridge been deserted all this time? Ebenezer had been too cold and preoccupied to care. But just as the genius made this pronouncement, one great yellow cab lumbered into view. As it rolled to a stop just feet from them, she saw the empty driver's seat.

"See, Ebenezer, there's a lot of perks to being me," the city said as she maneuvered the groaning man into the back seat. "Free Yankees tickets, all the food I could ever eat, and no waiting ever!"

With a laugh, she slammed the door and stepped around the purring vehicle.

"And there's perks for you, too. See, I was gonna make you walk in the snow and cold all the way out to our next meeting, just to be an asshole. So thank Tim here for changing our plans." Mock-bowing low, she opened the other passenger door. "Get in—the fare's on me."

As the cab maneuvered Brooklyn's spotty Christmas Eve traffic, Ebenezer scolded herself for not changing into sweatpants as she rubbed her goose-bumped legs.

"Can you turn the heat up?" she called to New York City, who now occupied the driver's seat as if she did this kind of thing each day. Maybe she did.

"Spare no luxury, huh?" But the back seat's vents spewed artificial warmth soon enough.

Ebenezer mumbled thanks as she stared out the window at the lowering city. She had visited Brooklyn several times—at least, enough to recognize its theaters and affordable apartments—and its flat-lined sky always made her feel too young and exposed.

"Gee, this night's just full of surprises," she grumbled.

New York City laughed as she took a corner a little too fast.

"We haven't even begun!"

Ebenezer opened her mouth to give what she knew would be a perfect comeback, cutting and witty. But a gurgling moan from the other passenger cut her off and lost the jibe forever.

"What?" Ebenezer turned to face the man.

He was fat in the way of middle age and office jobs, and scant-haired, the little bit remaining wispy as weeds and lacquered by the snow and what appeared to be egg yolks. He was brown, and the kind of wan only high fluorescent lights and exhausted social lives could produce. His suit was bargain basement, faded and rumpled like the rest of him.

He moaned again, and his eyelids lifted; beneath the bloodshot and the rheum, he had the brownest eyes she had ever seen.

"Why didn't you let me do it?" he whimpered, childlike. Not dazed, Ebenezer realized, but drunk.

Spirits—or whatever they had been back there—probably tended to have that effect on a person, she figured. His breath was rank with vodka, bourbon, and the sweet rot of tequila. He was lucky to be alive, and would have one hell of a hangover for Christmas. Although, that was ostensibly better than bloating under ice.

"Tim. Is your name Tim?" She did not know why she bothered. What was one more suicide to the world and its surplus population?

The eyelids fluttered. The man nodded and said yes.

"What are we doing with him, again?" Ebenezer asked.

Behind the Plexiglas divider, New York City sang along with some tuneless Christmas carol and pretended not to hear her even (and especially, Ebenezer thought angrily) when she pounded on it with her fist.

"Jackass," she said, slumping back into her seat. It took her a full five seconds to notice that Tim was clutching her hand. "Let go!"

He held on tighter.

"Let the fuck go!"

But his grip was firm, as if he had already tumbled from the bridge and changed his mind as the water met him. When he made no perverted move to stroke her knuckles or reach higher, Ebenezer sighed and let her hand rest on her thigh.

The cab slushed along the roads; the snow drifted down like dandelion seeds. She sucked her lip and blushed in rage and misery. What did you say to someone who had reached out for death? What did you even say?

She thought of her mother.

"It's all right," she said, knowing full well that it wasn't. "It's going to be all right."

"It won't." Tim's voice was gray and hollow as a cracked bell. Happily or not, it tolled on brokenly. "I thought it would all work out. I married Ann. Then I had kids, and then I got the MBA after everything they threw against me.

"But it doesn't work. Not ever." His voice broke like a storm, and his fingernails gouged deep. "I want to go back," he whimpered. "It's not enough. *I'm* not enough. It wasn't supposed to be like this. None of it."

Ebenezer's blood ran through her like knives. Before she could think better of it, she had spoken.

"I could have said that. I…I could have…"

Tim's gaze met hers, and his eyes seemed to focus.

"What's your name?" he asked at last.

On one of her many Salt Lake City hospital visits, Aunt Vona had taken her to the public library because "Good Lord! The poor child needs a break from all this death and dying business!" In a heavy brown-covered book, Ebenezer had read of fairies and the importance of not speaking names. It had been good preparation for life in any city.

It had also been the reason, she suspected, that a 22-year-old girl named Hadar Rishkin had become Bellwether, costumer and performance artist for parties, birthdays and alternative bat mitzvahs then, subsequently Bell.

The difference? The fairies' reasoning had been wise and self-defensive. Bell's, as ever, had been asinine.

You just couldn't trust your name or any details to a stranger, unless he or she—and he, especially—gave you a card that said *Director*. And even then...

"Ebenezer," she said gently.

"Ebenezer," he repeated with that drunken thoughtfulness. He looked so tired and broken, too much so to say what he wanted, what he needed. So, she sighed and said it for him.

"Hey."

This time New York City answered her knock.

"Yo."

"Take him home. Hurry."

"And if his family thinks he's the loser freak he says he is?"

"You know where he lives!" Ebenezer snapped. "And how many times do I have to tell you to shut the hell up? They'll deal. I know," she said, folding his hand in her thin fingers as if it were a secret. "I know." She sighed again. "Though I don't know why the hell I'm doing this."

Only she did, and knew it. But looking at the reason hurt.

"Just stop arguing and do it," she said.

"All right, relax. We're practically there already." And soon enough, New York City eased the car against the curb in a parallel job that even Ebenezer had to applaud, although she did so silently.

The cab's doors opened on a dim and cluttered neighborhood that 1980 had lacked the ability or will to leave. Garbage bags sogged darkly along sidewalks someone had abandoned in mid-salt, most likely too dispirited by the snow's resemblance to vomit to continue. The neighborhood had an incomplete appearance, and the old apartments hunched down upon each other as if in realization that togetherness was their only strength in sickness.

Without a word, the genius of New York City scooped Tim into her flashing arms and conveyed him through one of the slouching doors. This time, Ebenezer grabbed on to her mantel just in time to avoid another mishap with another door.

The hallways were just as tired as their exteriors. The corridor lights glowed and pulsed half-heartedly, as if nobody could possibly enter whose safety would be their concern. The carpeting stank of mildew and something like wet welcome mats.

"And I thought I lived in a dump," Ebenezer tried to joke. New York City did not have to roll her eyes for her to know how flat the attempt fell.

"He really must be bad off," she tried again, doing her best to sound clinical, observant.

"Isn't everyone these days?"

"Yeah, but…"

But she was right. Everybody worked jobs they hated, came home to lovers they despised and kids that screamed and things that never worked out like they should have. She told herself the same thing every day, and every day the words made her feel as if her skin had grown too small.

She followed the genius up a flight of stairs that twisted like a Byzantine mosaic. Somehow, she knew the black door to her right belonged to him even before the genius eased Tim to the floor and propped him there like an abandoned doll.

Not knowing why she did it, Ebenezer removed her coat and draped it over him like a blanket.

"Not necessary," New York City said as she rapped one great knuckle against the wood. "They're home, and he'll be warm and fussed over soon enough, just like you thought."

"That's not the point."

But she was hard-pressed to find what was as she tucked the garment over his shoulders. Somewhere between the sidewalk and the hall, Tim's dark eyes had closed, and now he breathed deeply and malodorously. No matter how his wife and children tried, she suspected he would spend the rest of Christmas Eve doing just that.

"Okay, he's good," the genius said, as if that ended everything. "Lucky for us, our next appointment lives right across from him."

A day ago—an hour or two ago—Ebenezer might have been surprised. Now she couldn't help but laugh.

"And I bet you planned it out exactly that way."

"In me, everything is well-constructed chaos. You know how it is."

She beckoned to the door across the hall. Groaning, Ebenezer followed with a last glance at Tim, thinking that she heard the lock of his apartment grind. He would be fine, she reassured herself. And so, back to the present.

"Now that we've seen my boss's fascinating life and saved someone else's, can we please stop visiting random people?"

"Of course! But this person's not exactly random."

"Oh, who is it? The director of that production of *The Seagull* I did at college? I haven't seen her for six years, but sure! Let's see what she's been up to! Or maybe Bell? I barely know her, but I'd love to watch whatever weird Czech stop-motion films she's got in her Netflix queue!"

New York City only clicked her pneumatic tongue and tugged her through the scabby door.

"Or maybe my manager at McDonald's when I graduated," Ebenezer sneered as they emerged in the cramped living room beyond. "Or maybe even—"

A girl wearing a pirate bandana ploughed through them.

Scene V

Debt

"Yar-har-haaaar, me hearties!"

For the second time that night, Ebenezer staggered from the onslaught and banged her elbow hard against the wall.

"You little shit!" she shouted at the child, who was now jumping on a tattered sofa, her blond hair streaming from her head; like the ocean, it was all in waves. The cushions dipped precariously, and with them a bespectacled boy and his thick book, the covers of which he snapped shut as he focused a glare of pure vitriol upon the interloper.

"Gra-aand-maa! Claire's *jumping* again!"

"Mo-om! Paul's *reading* again!" The girl—Claire, Ebenezer surmised—landed on her butt and scampered over to the boy. "Don't be boring!" she declared, slapping at his book. "And don't call Mom Grandma, either! That's rude!"

"Cut it out, Claire!"

"Make me, stupid!"

The boy scooted away like a crab, a gesture Ebenezer knew quite well; it meant he had a geyser steaming in him. It would not be pretty.

106

"Arrr! Arrr! Ye be goin' to walk the plank!" Claire prodded with both sword and voice.

"Go. Away!"

"Cut it out! Both of you!"

Ebenezer pivoted at the sound of the familiar voice.

A mountain of a woman sat ten feet away in an easy chair that, like the rest of the apartment, had seen far better days. Her blue housecoat cut off at mid-calf, the legs below slipperless and so swollen with edema Ebenezer was unsurprised to note their bareness. From the information her call sheets provided, she knew the woman was only 48, but the diseases ravaging her heart and brain made 60 seem generous.

"Martha Cratchit?"

New York City grinned.

"Told you it wasn't someone random."

Claire rolled onto her back, her blond hair spilling to the floor.

"But, Mo-om! He won't play."

"I'm reading," Paul informed her from behind his book. When Claire groaned and slapped at it again, he turned his back to her.

"He's reading on Christmas! Tell him not to?"

"If he wants to read Uncle Peter's present, let him. It's his Christmas, too."

"Told you," Paul huffed.

Claire frowned. "Nobody around here's any fun."

"Well, that's us old people for you," Martha's chair popped fiercely as the mountain of her shifted. "Watch the TV."

"There's nothing but the stupid Grinch. Or that one shitty show about the mouse and the stupid clock."

107

"Watch your mouth, Claire."

The girl snorted, billowing her bangs.

"Sorry. But it's true! It *is* a shitty show."

"And y'know, Florence and Dad'll be home with dinner any time now. If you're that put off, you can go set the table."

The child sat up straight quickly, insisting, "No, I'm fine."

Martha chuckled. "Yeah, I thought so. Cheer up. Maybe Flo'll play pirates with you when she's home, if you ask nice."

Sighing, the girl plodded across and flopped down again at her...mother's?...swollen feet.

"Tell me a story? About pirates. Or when you were little in Florida? Or maybe pirates in Florida!"

"There are no pirates in Florida!" Paul insisted without looking up. "At least, not anymore."

Claire stuck out her tongue.

"I meant pretend," she explained, followed by a raspberry. The boy—her brother?—returned the courtesy.

"Claire, be nice and leave him alone, or bed with no dessert."

"Sorry, Mom. He's just an annoying brother."

Ebenezer caught herself smiling. Claire's exuberance and bright-eyed wit was infectious. There was a familiarity about her, like a crush of shag carpet on bare forearms, or snowfall observed through a broad window.

"Oh," she whispered.

But as Claire plopped onto her belly and picked up two scattered toys—a pirate ship and a headless Bar-

108

bie—Ebenezer hardened her smile into a grimace. There was no use in being wistful. Life would snuff her out soon enough.

Doll and ship in hand, the girl propped her chin on the chair's arm.

"Mom? Tell me why you got sick, then? If we can't talk about pirates."

Ebenezer expected Martha to launch into a tirade, as she always did on the phone when confronted with her debts from diabetes, or the withering heart in her large bosom. Instead, one bloated hand carded the girl's hair.

"That's a sad story, child, and not one I really understand. The doctors said it's 'cause Nana also had heart disease, and because some people in my family had diabetes, but nobody really knows what makes it happen when it does. Sometimes, you're just going on living and things happen."

"Like how our last dad kept getting in trouble, so you're our mom now and Robert's our dad now?"

"Yeah, I guess. A lot of life's like that. But there's also family and friends and hot chocolate and Christmas Eve—"

"And pirates!"

"Mhm. Though I don't really like them as much as you."

"Nobody does," Paul said from his place on the sofa. And surprisingly, all three of them laughed.

Ebenezer found she was smiling again. Promptly, she fought the feeling back.

"Right. So, the girl has ADD, and the boy's probably going to kill her before New Year's. Charming domestic scene." She rolled her eyes. "But do we really have to watch it?"

"Hmm, let's see. About five hours ago, you swore at this woman and said you'd call the po-pos on her. So I kind of think you do."

"I was just doing my job."

"I don't really need to point out why that excuse is shit, do I?"

"There's no law against collecting money that people owe!"

"And no matter how many times you repeat that, it won't make you sleep any better. Look, I'm New York City," she said when Ebenezer's mouth popped into a surprised O. "I see how you grit your teeth when you do it. I even feel your heart beat faster."

"Listen, I do not make half of what I need, yet somehow *I* manage to pay my debts."

"I think you really want me to hit your mouth before this is over," the genius snapped. "I don't get you, kid. You don't like your harassing her any more than she does, so why do you do it?"

"We've all got to eat," Ebenezer said, feeling quite scalded. "And you do what you have to."

"Well, so does she."

The apartment door swung open, and two snowy people stamped inside. One was a woman close to Ebenezer's age with Claire's blond waves and her mother's chin. The other was a man who looked far closer to his mid-40s than the woman Ebenezer guessed was his spouse. Both were carrying paper and plastic bags from which the smells of tomatoes, herbs, and starches wafted like clouds.

"Hi, Mom," the woman chirped as she placed her load on the scratched kitchen counter.

She swung off her scarf and unbuttoned her coat, revealing black slacks and a messy apron beneath which round breasts bloomed and wide hips curved, both suggesting Martha's might have looked the same twenty years ago.

"Sorry we're late. I put out the closed sign, and there was this couple that just would *not* take the hint! Like every night."

"And then they were out of angel hair, so Florence had to make up more," the man added as he, too, shucked off his coat. He was balding, slight, the kind of man Ebenezer always imagined attending folk festivals and trying to comfort his inner child. He wore a well-pressed suit that did not fit with the apartment, and his gold name tag boasted ROBERT and the Art Nouveau logo of the Broadstairs Hotel Chain—a beach curling into forever.

"Yay! Dinner!" Claire rushed into the dingy kitchenette to help her adopted sister unpack the Styrofoam tubs of spaghetti, ravioli, garlic bread, and salad—which, naturally, meant getting in the way more often than not.

After some mental gymnastics, Ebenezer gave up on determining the exact relationship between a woman's daughter and her adopted nephews and nieces. It felt pointless.

The boy curled on the sofa like a shrimp, probably wanting to be there even less than the interloper did. So he stayed as daughters and husband bustled and mother sat like a continent. Take-out tops sprung

111

like jaws, the lids of sauce tubs belched indecorously as they revealed meaty marinara, dribbly garlic, and sloughs of alfredo that Ebenezer had always found about as appetizing as warm snot. Florence assigned a plate of steamed vegetables and "low-carb option" linguini to Martha, who rolled her eyes in mock irritation and insisted carbohydrates were the only thing she missed about being her eldest daughter's age.

Then, they were all about the quaint business of mastication and Christmas Special-viewing.

"The old folks at home," Ebenezer muttered.

New York City responded by flicking her nose soundly.

As far as interesting happenings went, that was just about it for half an hour. The Heat and Cold Misers distracted Claire from pirates, and Paul, looking heated, turned his pages. Plastic TV trays were pulled apparently from nowhere, and Martha, Robert, and Florence ate in a row, speaking of this dreadful customer or that long line.

And was Mom feeling better than this morning? And this family from, God, Michigan, who could *not* have a room near elevators because it might cause cancer. And then, whispered and all-too-briefly after Florence herded the children into the bedroom with promises of early presents, *Had* Belinda called?

"Well, I guess I can't say I'm surprised," Robert sighed when Martha shook her graying head mournfully. "No other calls from Kentucky, right?"

"Nope. No parole officers, hers or her boyfriend's. Oh. Pete did call to wish us Merry Christmas and to talk to the kids a bit." The sad smile made Martha's face look like an onion.

Ebenezer raised one unplucked eyebrow. So, they also had a Ronelle.

"He misses uncle time, I think. In person," Martha continued, in the tone of someone slapped too much. "Wish we could have him out here sometime. Louisville's so flat and cold this time a year. Just like a rust bucket. Not that here's any better."

"He won't mind the mess, honey."

"Nah, it's not that. Just want him to remember me before…" She flexed her fingers like picking up balls, moved her rippling arms out wide, encompassing herself.

Robert took one swollen hand and clutched it.

"Don't say that. Nothing's going to happen."

Martha shrugged and shook her head again.

"You know who makes the decisions. And you'll love this, too—another collection call from that little bitch."

Ebenezer swallowed.

Robert's body jerked backwards, as if the very notion could burn him.

"On Christmas *Eve*?"

"Three-fifteen p.m.! It's on the caller ID." Martha watched Rudolph's mohair legs twitch across the paper sky as her face contorted. "She calls once, twice, one day three times, and someone calls all evening till I cry and yell at the kids."

Her eyes were reddening and already glossed with tears.

"I know, Martha, I know," Robert said, as if confessing his uselessness to help. Ebenezer wondered if he felt chained, like the ghosts and memories and the

113

other detritus of misery she had glimpsed upon the bridge.

"I'd record them, but the machine's busted, and it wouldn't do no good. Cops got better things than that."

"Honey..."

"And if they're telling the truth, and there's a warrant, well..." Her hands spread wide again. "What are they going to do? Jail'd at least have medical care—maybe."

"Well, that would be better than my job," her husband tried, the smile on his face so very, very brave.

Martha took one look, and it was like a reservoir rupturing. Tears and snot tumbled across the valleys of her ruddy face as her hands tried to muffle the explosion from the children in the bedroom—the only bedroom, Ebenezer realized as the door swung open on Florence's backside.

"Fifteen more minutes, then it's dessert time," she called before shutting the door.

She took in the image of her weeping mother in her father's arms, and her smile sloughed instantly into a well-weathered grimace.

"Oh, Mom." Her soft arms were tight around Martha's shoulders almost before the rest of her could finish the trek. "Mom, it's Christmas."

"'Your debt doesn't take a vacation.' That's what she said."

Ebenezer bit her lip to hear her own words thrown back like a snowball spiked with ice.

"And the kids were right there—and they had questions. Especially Paul. He's always been so bright. He just looked at me when I didn't say much, shrugged, and went back to his book, and sometimes I think he hates me."

Florence's arms pulled tighter.

"No. No."

"His mom says she's just going out for some cigarettes, so just sit right there and watch the baby. Two days later, he hears a car, and it's DCFS. Belinda says she loves her angel babies so much then signs them over.

"It's just lies and more lies for him. He don't hardly talk these days, except when Claire's bothering him." She wiped her face messily on her sleeve. "I'm sorry. You're both right. It's Christmas. But sometimes I just don't…It's been a bad year," she concluded.

"I know, Mom." Florence kissed her cheek. "But I'm here. The Da Vinci Bowl is doing fine, and maybe I'll make sous chef next year. Even in this economy. And no, I do not mind loaning you money. In fact, I want to," she insisted when Martha moved to protest. "It's like paying you back for culinary school. If you have to think of it as something besides love."

"Generous, smart, and she cooks like the restaurant's namesake—a grand master of Italian cuisine!"

"Dad," Florence protested, blushing, but somewhat gratefully, in Ebenezer's opinion.

"Yeah. We've got a good daughter there," Martha agreed.

Robert pulled a handkerchief out from some impossible pocket in his starched uniform and gave it to his wife. Then, clutching her hand harder, he kissed her cheek, her lips, her eyes.

"I hate that there's nothing to say that doesn't sound helpless or empty. But we're still here. Us, Flo, the kids.

It's not perfect, but we're here. For now. And it's Christmas, and there are good things on TV and Flo's awesome—in the word's classical sense—food from all the way uptown. It's just beginning to snow. And I love you."

But neither of them said *You'll be fine* or *We're going to survive*.

And then Claire returned in a flail of limbs, hair, and energy, and her brother plodded after, suckling a candy cane and ears-deep in a book Ebenezer swore was different than the one he'd had before.

In the same way everything had unpinned itself, it all settled back down. The family laughed and chattered, and the snow fell in great white puffs as each did his or her best to ignore the fear and want pulling at their faces with fierce tenacity.

Ebenezer tilted her head, considering.

"New York? Cratchit…Martha. Is she going to be all right?"

"Yeah, what Robert said. For now."

"No, I mean…she looks like hell." She sucked her lip. Even she could not say it.

The genius shrugged, but not unkindly.

"See, I deal with the present. Twenty million people, more with tourists. Who knows how many miles above and underground and in the air? I'm always changing, usually too fast to look. But, since you asked, the future's like a tombstone in a mortician's lot—it's cold, and not yet written. Real cold."

Ebenezer tasted copper and wondered how that had happened. How everything had happened.

"Good job, by the way, at making their Christmas just a little happier," the genius said, as casually as if she were discussing the weather.

Ebenezer had to look away.

"Anyhow, we're done here."

She had never thought of Martha's face. Not really. Not beyond cartoons. The way she struggled through her smiles and looked so pale, and so familiar...

"Wait."

But the genius grabbed her shoulder as she tried to cross the room.

"Cab's waiting, sugar cheeks. And trust me—I want to get this shit over more than you."

That said, Ebenezer was dragged backwards through the door and into the mildewing hallway; a glance at the apartment opposite showed a locked and battered door, no Tim in sight. Her coat, however, slumped on the floor like a shrugged-off shadow. As Ebenezer buttoned it, she thought she caught a hint of desperation.

The whole place reeked of it.

Scene VI

Want and Ignorance

Neither genius nor woman said a thing as they tucked themselves into the waiting taxi, and the silence settled heavy as a blanket as their equipage crawled through the slush and chill.

Huddling in the artificial heat, Ebenezer counted the storefronts and the passers-by. Each blended into the darkness like brushstrokes in an Impressionist's failed experiment.

But sometimes, she caught a glimpse.

A crown of tight-spun curls reminded her of Right from work. What was her name, and where was she tonight? In another hideous apartment where the radiator bleated, or in the bed of a bright hotel room with a lover, maybe two?

A man with skin like leather and wearing a tattered coat hefted a crying girl into his arms. Had she just skinned her knee on the sidewalk, and would there be comfort and cocoa in some homeless shelter?

Three girls of two races laughed past a grated building, hands locked in the way that always telegraphs heterosexuality—college students? An English, psychology, and quantum physics major, respectively?

118

"Just pensive," she explained when New York City remarked upon her silence. She wanted to see Marley more than ever, but somehow, she could not find the energy to ask.

In this way, she traveled back across the bridge, now phantomless and seeming eerily deserted. She leaned her head against the window as the cab splashed into Alphabet City, where the clubs cast bands of green, pink, and Prussian blue against the snow's descending curtain. When younger, she had regarded them with a mixture of suspicion and contempt, and now she felt they were too young to draw her interest.

All were, of course, haunted. In one neon building, she and Marley had ordered so many New Year's drinks neither could explain the Japanese paper fans or the chains of paperclips jammed into their coat pockets the next morning. In another, they had fled an agonizing concert to kiss and kiss on overstuffed lounge couches.

Oh, yes, she knew why memories haunted. Exactly.

The cab rumbled around a dark, familiar corner, and there was The Well, its cords of lavender fairy lights perpetually serpentining around its awning, seasonally appropriate at last. The sight of its glittering windows and the couples, threesomes and moresomes spilling from its doors recovered Ebenezer's voice.

"We are *not* going in there."

"I know that, thanks." The cab obediently stopped at a red light, and the genius turned, a headline about the "worst snow storm this year" trickling across her left cheek. "Why? You need a drink or something?"

"Before tonight's over, I might." Ebenezer scanned the sidewalks, reminding herself that Marley had not liked this place since that very public argument. "We used to come here every Friday, if we didn't have work or rehearsals. Though it was pretty much always rehearsals for Marley—or some show."

A sweep of red drew her attention. The ghosts were back.

From the hint of furrows on her brow, Ebenezer guessed her image was roughly twenty-five, but the discontent that had hung about her then was hidden well enough behind a smile. As she stood with one arm around her girlfriend's waist, Marley groaned and threw her head back, growling with frustration as she let out a mighty sneeze. In the fuzzy amber light thrown by the street lamps, Ebenezer saw the fever in her cheeks and on her brow; her face looked like a half-ripened cherry.

Marley sneezed again and coughed the phlegm down gracelessly.

"Ohhh, why are there never any cabs when you need them?"

"For the same reason life exists—to piss us off."

Marley snorted. "Somehow, I don't think we're the center of their universes."

"And that's the problem."

Marley's black lace camisole had ridden up during her stretch, exposing a hill of a belly almost as pale as salt. Ebenezer's slender fingers slid against it, rubbed in little circles.

"I remind you that I said this wasn't the best top for January and a cold."

"Mh. Thanks, Mom." Marley chuckled as she leaned into the touch. One arm lazily stretched up and looped around Ebenezer's neck. "Well, now they probably won't stop because we look really drunk. And really gay."

"Except we're not." Ebenezer kissed through her hair. "Uh. The first one, anyway."

Marley snorted, knotting her fingers over her girlfriend's knuckles and closing her eyes. In the cab's back seat, Ebenezer bit her lip, remembering the smell of orchids, coat lint, Marley—uniquely Marley.

"You know, I really love you," she said—right before her head turned and a burst of milky snot covered her girlfriend's coat.

Ebenezer regarded it with a drollness her older self could not remember ever having felt. Perhaps Marley did not recognize it, either; when Ebenezer laughed, she pulled away with all her sickly strength.

"It's not funny! Damn it, it's not fucking funny!" She coughed up again. "If I can't sing through this, that's it."

"Well, I did tell you we should probably stay home."

"I was just sniffling when we left! I didn't know I—" Marley coughed again. "And you're not really helping. Just—stop scolding me and get a cab!"

"I know. I didn't mean to scold," Ebenezer said with a calm her future incarnation did not remember, either, as her hands moved to her girlfriend's heated face. "I just want to get you there as soon as possible, so you can have some tea and go to sleep. That's all. I'm sorry."

Marley tried to answer, but her face crumpled like a paper bag.

"God," she sniffled, approaching tears. "Oh, God. No, I should be the one that's sorry. It's just—it doesn't

121

stop. You know leads can't get sick. Not even during rehearsals. It's practically in the contract. And Nanami is just waiting for one fuck-up so she can get the actress she w—" She snuffled back a sneeze. "...she really wants." She leaned her wet face on her girlfriend's shoulder and caught her breath. "I'm sorry. I'm really...like you really need to hear me whining after what you've been through."

Ebenezer's older self agreed. Almost a year without a callback had made her less than sympathetic.

"Yeah, poor baby," she sneered at the ghost of Marley.

The Ebenezer of four years past frowned a little, thinking the same thing. But it shifted easily into a kiss on Marley's scaly lips.

"Oh, don't. I'm so gross."

But Ebenezer kissed her once again, and Marley leaned into it, sighing.

"I don't think a cab is coming, Ebbie. Except for the ones that are already taken."

"Story of my life," Ebenezer grunted. "It's three blocks to the subway, forty minutes home with the transfer. You're not waiting that long."

"So, are you going to, like, force one to stop with a finger gun or something?"

Ebenezer rolled her eyes in mock irritation.

"That pizzeria across the street is open. Go buy a drink and wait for me. When I flag one down, I'll wave. You can walk okay, right?"

Marley rolled her eyes, too.

"Whatever this is doesn't affect my legs. Not yet, at least."

"Hey," Ebenezer called, unbuttoning her coat as her girlfriend turned. "Here."

Marley caught it, green eyes widening.

"But…"

"You need it more. Go on."

"Right. Okay."

The two women smiled at each other before Ebenezer stepped from the curb and raised two fingers in the universal summons for a cab. Marley shuffled out of view, her lithe arms slipping easily into the black wool sleeves. Her teeth already gritted, Ebenezer realized she was beautiful, and lucky…and it hurt.

The light changed, and the cab departed, leaving the mist to swirl the streets. Ebenezer could not explain why she felt the need to speak, or to justify herself, especially to New York City.

Nonetheless, she told the genius, "I stood out there for twenty minutes. I timed it. Marley drank two Seven-Ups and lasted through rehearsals and a two-month run.

"I, on the other hand, came down with whatever flu from Hell she had and lost my job due to 'abusing sick days.'" Ebenezer made the quotes with her fingers before defensively nestling back into the seat. "Great metaphor for our relationship, right? She gets to coast, I get to deal with all the bullshit."

"You're right. I don't get why women don't just adore you."

"Thanks. They don't."

"Does that cross ever get boring?"

"Nope," Ebenezer trilled.

Surprisingly, that seemed to end it.

Neither spoke as the cab crept up the slushy avenue to Midtown and turned down a street braced up with scaffolding. It braked at the entrance to a small theatre that appeared to have been carved out of the feldgrau architecture long ago as a bakery or brothel, condemned twice, then resurrected as one of the not-for-profit spaces that dotted the island like migrating butterflies—or tumors, in Ebenezer's view. A dingy sign read *Chapman Theatre*; only the first T's silhouette remained. Outside, a few people in outlandish clothes—including one giant lobster—huddled smoking.

Ebenezer recognized the building long before the cab's engine shuttered off and wondered why she was not running. Too late—New York City was already opening the back door.

"I thought you'd like a little break."

"So you bring me to the place where I had my last gig. Thanks. Thanks a lot." But seeing no other choice, Ebenezer stepped from the vehicle, rubbing her hands together. Gloves, she decided, would be her next big splurge. "Anyway, you said you wanted to get this over with."

The genius nodded her crowned head as a train roared in a circle around her neck.

"Believe me, sweetie. I do. You don't check your answering machine."

"It's just Mom and some telemarketers. You should know."

"And somebody named Bell."

"Look, I don't know why she calls me. We did a reading here—some awful play by some awful teenager from New Jersey that still paid well—and she thought we should keep in touch. Marley thought it was a good idea, and I didn't really care. But she's..."

Ebenezer waved her hands, too many words coming to mind at once.

"Not worth a returned phone call? A fuck you? What?"

Ebenezer settled on "Annoying. Pretentious. Clueless. Stupid. Immature."

"So, *not* worth a returned phone call or a fuck you, then."

"She's a twenty-two-year-old performance artist. 'No' and 'fuck you' aren't in her vocabulary—at least outside of some weird sex sketch. When a kid's the only person who calls, it's just sad." Ebenezer rubbed her arms and shivered. "Why are we here?"

An advertisement for Coca-Cola flickered across one enormous black-lit cheek.

"If you'd check your messages like a human being, you'd know this is where the party's at."

Ebenezer did a double-take and scoffed, "Here? In this dump?"

The genius sucked her lips.

"Mhn. You can take the girl out of Utah, but apparently the party scene's too big a stretch."

Ebenezer, however, was not listening.

"It's a black box theatre! No stage, no curtains, they bring the chairs in for each performance..." She tugged the great door's weathered brass handle and started when it opened.

"Thought you didn't care about some kid's party," New York City called as her charge disappeared inside.

"How does it feel to be wrong, bitch?" Ebenezer muttered.

The empty lobby greeted her, the fluorescents buzzing greenly overhead like flies struck with ennui. A gentle upward slope for wheelchair users' ease led to a pair of worn-down doors; like the theatre beyond they were stained black. Someone had taped up two posters, each a painful explosion of color and language. Someone also, apparently, was obsessed with spaceships, chintz,

---

(You're Almost There!)

BELL'S NOT-CHANUKAH, NOT-CHRISTMAS, NOT-EID, NOT-DIWALI, NOT-KWANZAA

AGNOSTIC-STRAVAGANZA!!!!

IS JUST AHEAD!

WHAT EARTHLY DELIGHTS AND ARCANE PLEASURES AWAIT BEYOND THESE DOORS?!

(Note: BYO boas, bling, and b-movies, not booze, barbiturates or glitter—blue, burgundy, brown or bistre! It's a bitch to sweep up, and it shows all over black!)

— *BELL (YOUR BOUNTIFUL BENEFACTRESS)*

---

midnight movies, lasers, and the color mauve.

Ebenezer shook her head. "Twee."

"Unlike every twenty-two-year-old in the world," New York City said, peering over her shoulder. Once again, her dimensions had inexplicably shrunk to fit the room.

Suddenly, Ebenezer's hands felt too big and her stomach too empty. Something writhed deep within it, like a lobster in a dim and dripping cellar; her hand upon the brass door handle had frozen solid.

"They can't see me if you're there, right?"

"Anxious about crashing the kid's party? No. Remember? You're like the city when you're with me—nowhere and everywhere at once."

"Okay."

And if the genius questioned how her free hand had wound itself through the shimmering draperies of her robe, Ebenezer resolved to dismiss it as not wanting to get lost in the revelers—all five of them.

Why had Bell rented out a theatre? And how?

With her torch, New York City threw wide the doors, and five became fifteen, fifty, a few breaths away from one hundred, of every race and sex, every costume from the unimaginative to the ostentatious. Ebenezer's jaw and eyebrows fled from each other in surprise.

A human-sized candle waddled by. Seven more followed, each wrapped liberally in what seemed to be egg-crate foam and crowned with crimson cellophane that fluttered courtesy of some unseen mechanisms.

"Menorah!" called a woman's robust voice. "Where's my menorah?"

Every candle turned, narrowly avoiding a domino effect.

A great woman clad in black satin breeches and a silver-trimmed vest parted the guests as if they were the Red Sea. When Ebenezer had last seen her at one of Marley's shows two months ago, her hair had been a mess of black-and-green curls. Now, it was a spiky mess of black and magenta mashed under a tiny sparkling top hat held fast by a ruby-headed hatpin.

She had a round olive-tinted face and a smile that could have circumnavigated a globe; had Ebenezer not known her age, she would have guessed twenty-five or twenty-six.

She carried a clipboard in her bare left arm, which bore a tattoo of a haunted, closed-eyed face that looked to be a door knocker. Beneath it was *genug*, the Yiddish for the word *enough*, a fact she had explained when Marley asked for a translation. Ebenezer still didn't understand its significance.

The candles leaned in as Bell touched the tallest and the shortest on what must have been their shoulders.

"There you are! Hey, guys? If everyone's done the pictures, could you go to the boxing ring? Santa, the *tannenbaum*, and the manger are ready for round two, and Baby Jesus has some other thing to do at ten. The schmuck."

"Is that other thing Deepak?" the tallest candle asked with a grin that could only be called shit-eating.

Bell gasped in mock horror as she lightly slapped his cheek.

"Hey! You're the *shamash*! You do dirty talk like that, Tyrell, you break the *mitzvah*. And anyway, you're wrong. Deepak's doing a thing named Carl who couldn't come tonight because of a Queer Communist Worker's Party healthcare reform meeting or something."

The *shamash* candle—Tyrell—laughed, showing a very candle-like row of teeth.

"What?"

"'Pink is the New Red' is their slogan. True story. Or maybe that was some breast cancer program. Anyway." She spatted the candle's ass with her clipboard. "Get outta here. Christmas is up by one, and if Chanukah loses I'm out fifty bucks!"

Promising to win one for the Maccabees, the candles trundled off.

Standing on her tiptoes, Ebenezer saw a Santa Claus as obviously female as she was padded sending up rude gestures like smoke signals.

"You wanna piece a me?"

The candles returned the favor, trying not to capsize as their fingers rose in the New York salute. Soon they had vanished in the crowd. Grinning, Bell walked in the opposite direction towards a table heaped with a UN's-worth of food.

The cast of *The Rocky Horror Picture Show* flittered past, followed by a woman in a blue sequined gown from which twenty Styrofoam goldfish swam on wires. She was deep in conversation with a skinny Buddha Ebenezer recognized as Deepak.

In fact, she at least vaguely recognized most of the brightly costumed revelers—mostly acquaintances from gala nights, auditions, art galleries, and long-ago productions.

And Marley's legion of friends. Even knowing she was currently as unremarkable to them as air, Ebenezer felt like hiding in a corner.

Bell was at the long table laughing with two blond women in red and green flapper dresses strewn with fairy lights as she piled potatoes on their paper plates. "Try it! You'll love it!" At least, Ebenezer thought her full lips said as much. She did not know Red, but she remembered addressing the words *fuck* and *you* to Green a year ago, maybe, at one of Bell's obligatory parties when she had momentarily escaped Marley's supervision. She recalled no name, only an argument and the line of Marley's lips as she pulled her away.

Quite abruptly, her stomach rumbled, and Ebenezer realized two things—but for her fries and chicken nuggets, she had eaten nothing all day long, and the table was heaped with latkes, Badam Phirni, fruitcake, sugar cookies and—most thankfully—less sweet foods like fried fish, beef rendang, malhi kofta, basted turkey, yams and mashed potato islands in brown gravy and a rainbow of rice, salads, and fruit.

Her hunger and nothing else moved her forward, Ebenezer told herself. Her hunger and nothing more. She made no move to ask New York City's permission, and the genius, busy dangling her torch over two men hitting each other with down pillows, did not order her to stay.

When Bell moved off with the blinking flapper girls Ebenezer heaped a paper plate with fried chicken, lentils in rich butter sauce, duck-fat latkes, and all the vegetables she could balance. For twenty minutes, she had no thought but for grease and the crisp crunch of produce she had nearly forgotten.

The party's thrum became as distant as the dream she sometimes thought this strange evening must surely be. When she had finished, she expected to feel bloated, tired, excessive. Perversely, though, her arms and legs felt as if they'd lightened, and with them a little of the gloom that had settled down so heavily this last week.

Following Bell suddenly seemed like the best idea ever, and Ebenezer went along with the impulse after stiffly reminding herself that Marley's friends would not—could not—make an awkward mess of everything.

She did not know what powered Bell—drugs, a turnkey or just that enthusiasm that falls off by twenty-four—but Bell simply did not saunter. Oh, she moved everywhere among her guests, but not to question them like a waitress offering a refill.

Here, she stopped to congratulate a man and woman dressed in *Star Trek* uniforms on the bouncing Tribble-baby in the man's arms. ("Three months already! So hard to believe. You're bringing her to not-Valentine's Day, right?")

There, she stepped with more grace than her body should have possessed from the path of a wheelchair decked out like a steam-powered sleigh then leaned down to hug its stiff-faced occupant, who grinned immediately. ("Mariam, I was so worried when I heard about your foot! You look great! Oh, sorry. Let me check on the living statue garden, then we'll talk. For Christ's sake, the way they go through silver paint!")

Here, making a round through seven metal-hued and frozen people and pronouncing them "just fabulous." There, admiring an in-progress sand painting briefly before excusing herself back to the wheelchair and its owner, now seated on a brocade sofa Ebenezer vaguely recalled from a shabby production of *The Importance of Being Earnest* Marley had dragged her to.

Here. There. Here. There. Here. It made Ebenezer's lightening head feel even lighter.

When Bell at last settled on an equally ragged chair from the same show, Ebenezer eased onto the floor beside it, plate still in hand and well out of the way of the considerable foot traffic.

"Wow. Sorry! Next time I think I'm going to put a limit on the art exhibits—which means, of course, I'll just have more." She sighed dramatically. "But are you having fun?"

"It's a wonderful party," Mariam replied. Raising a cane Ebenezer had not noticed, she indicated a male angel, blindfolded, loin-clothed, and led by a female skeleton bearing a scythe as he dispensed fortune cookies to passers-by. "I like *him*."

Ebenezer cringed as Bell threw her head back, braying with laughter.

"Yeah, he gets that a lot. That winning ass…er, assets."

Mariam snorted and waved Bell closer.

"Move in. I can't hear you."

Bell shuffled her chair over.

"So, how is it? No more pain?"

"Eh. It comes and goes. Mostly stays." She shrugged. "What'cha gonna do?"

"Maybe get a sexy angel to do a body rub?"

The woman laughed. "Why not?"

With a wink, Bell was on her feet.

"Nikolai! Clea! Paging Nikolai and Clea. Nikolai and Clea, please come to the Half-Assed Burning Man

Art Lounge. We have a code blue massage; repeat, code blue!"

The angel and the skeleton were already on their way. His black curls slithered and bounced like graceful serpents, her afro spread down to her shoulders like Spanish moss. Ebenezer pursed her lips. She was certain she had never seen the woman before, but the man looked strangely familiar.

Nikolai…Nikolai…what? She bit into an apple slice. Why did she want to say Braginsky? Barakov?

As Clea settled on a stool painted to resemble a sunrise, Nikolai kissed Bell's proffered hand.

"Bella-Bell," he purred, his voice carrying just the faintest suggestion of Russian. "What is this I hear about a charming lady needing a back rub?" He winked at Clea, who rolled her eyes good-naturedly.

"Oh, just ignore him. I think he had a few too many Buds before we came."

"Shhh!" Nikolai put two fingers to her lips. "If word gets out that I like anything but wodka, Julliard might deport me." Somehow, his laugh was even mightier and more obnoxious than the hostess's.

Clea turned to Bell.

"Is he always like this?"

"Yeah. Just give him a month, you'll learn to tolerate it. Or recognize it, at least."

"Or love it!" Nikolai pecked his girlfriend on the lips. "So, Bell. Where does it hurt? The same shoulder as last time?"

"No, it's a foot. On me," Mariam held her leg aloft, then rested it on Bell's thigh.

"Ah! My apologies, madam. I didn't see you there."

133

"I get that a lot. Surprisingly," she replied, indicating her wheelchair.

The scowl carving up her face, the blush across Nikolai's cheeks like a slap—Ebenezer saw it all a second before it happened.

"And such a gorgeous sleigh!" the angel over-enthused. "Did you, ah, make it yourself?"

"No, the frigging elves did. Don't patronize me, kid."

"I didn't mean—"

"Right. Excuse me, Bell. I'm outta here."

"Wait!" The angel grabbed for her wheelchair as she reached for the stick, and the cane came up.

"Hands off, or I'll break your face. I don't care if you're her friend."

Bell appeared between them.

"Y'know, when I planned this party, I didn't think there'd be a cage fight between Gabriel the Archangel and Santa's sleigh. But it's got promise." She grinned.

All three guests stared at her incredulously. Then, a balloon seemed to deflate. To Ebenezer's surprise, Mariam was the first to laugh, then Nikolai, rubbing the back of his head and looking a bit confused, and Clea finally, unclenching on her seat like a loosened spring.

"I am really, really sorry," Nikolai explained when all began to catch their breaths. "I meant only that I know Bell and her shoulders well, and since I had not yet made your charming acquaintance…"

Mariam waved her hands like clearing away smoke.

"Yeah, I get it. It's okay. Let's just move on."

Nikolai nodded and crouched at her feet.

134

"Great! Which one seems to be troubling you, madam…?"

"Just Mariam. Mrs. Madam. Lady. They all make me feel damn old."

"Mariam, then."

Ebenezer watched the angel take the woman's feet out of her shoes and found her attention wandering, much like it had on the afternoon she was forced to watch the video of a live birth in freshman health class. The effect did not surprise her—massages had always seemed like messy business, all of that touching and muscles. Before her late supper could begin wriggling in her stomach, she turned her attention to Bell and Clea, who had launched into full blown conversation.

"So, what's the story in Clea land?"

"Same as always—dancing night and day and worrying if my master's will be worthless—or if there'll be any companies left in January."

"Hey, listen, recessions aren't like Chinese dynasties. They're more like clinical depression—you hit a low, it goes back up eventually. There'll be companies, and there'll be theaters, and there'll be books and movies and all that other stuff. People need pretty things just as much as they need food, maybe more. Just like clothes."

Bell gestured at her body.

"You know, Mom cried when I said a sewing machine was better than a man, and I was going to Tisch instead of NYU Law. She'd put me down for a lawyer the minute the doctor smacked my tuchas. Fast forward—I pay for a studio in Astoria and do regular radio things in between the stitching and the serging. Even the alternative bat mitzvahs are picking up."

"Yeah," Clea licked her teeth. "The hell are those, anyway?"

Bell shrugged. "You got me. They call, I go. And if I can make five hundred bucks making Becky look like Boston's catch of the day, the world's still turning."

Clea slipped her thin hands into Bell's palms.

"Thank you, by the way. Without that five hundred dollars—"

Bell shrugged. "Eh. I wanted to do it, I could. That's all. And I like your apartment. I hope you and him stay there." She waved in Nikolai's direction. Looking up from Mariam's red toenails, the dancer waved back.

"Did you just take my name in vain?"

"No, your girlfriend's just talking dirty about money." Bell turned back to the grim reaper. "How about I just don't give you any Chanukah *or* Christmas gifts for, oh, fifteen years?"

"Will you at least let me say a rosary?" her friend asked, brow furrowing just slightly.

"Oh, sure! I don't know if anyone'll hear it, but, hey, it can't hurt. Oh. When you do, tell the BVM I'm sorry for fucking up the hemline on her robe? And for using that Virgin of Guadalupe print instead of the Prussian blue? Well, if all else fails, just tell her it was on sale."

Clea snorted. "I'll see what I can do."

The conversation continued like that for several minutes: Bell's first Off-Broadway But Not Cheap commission; Clea's tarot readings that paid the couple's grocery bill, and the lives of several people Ebenezer knew only as acquaintances or vaguely through Marley. Mariam's illness that had weakened her joints and baffled her doctors; Tanya's amicable divorce; Alexander's art show last month; Raul's trip to Toronto—all stories she had never heard or, she wondered, ignored in the telling?

Yet Bell seemed to know them all by heart, not by rote. As she listened, Ebenezer recalled faces—gaunt Marlowe, the stage manager at that horrid reading where Bell first leaped into her life; Heather, who she remembered now as the woman wearing the foam fish—hadn't she seen her crying into a cell phone on 44th Street once, her mascara dribbling tragicomically? And he—had he mentioned volunteering for a cat rescue shelter?

For many years, these people had blown around her like yesterday's newspapers, just as substantial and important. Now, they had more depth than a millimeter, more breadth than the margins she had drawn.

Something prickled in her stomach. It felt very much like shame.

"Hey, Bell?"

Both women turned as a man in nothing but a golden halo and a cloth diaper called her name.

"Yes, M'Lord?"

The Baby Jesus smiled.

"My grandma would kill me if she knew I laughed at that. Just so you know, Chanukah beat Christmas two to one."

"Well, mazel-frickin-tov!"

"And like half of everybody want you to make a toast."

137

Bell puffed her cheeks and blew air through her lips in a sound just short of rude.

"What, they want a medal for that, too?"

From the couch, Mariam let out a little happy moan. Ebenezer noted Nikolai was now working on her shoulders.

Why did she smell the dim interior of a sound booth when she looked at him?

"I think they just want something off-the-cuff," the Baby Jesus said. "Nothing fancy."

"Well, then, they came to the wrong party! I memorized the whole thing this morning. Is the mic on stage working now?"

"Yeah, that guy dressed like Ded Moroz screwed it back together."

Bell tsked lightly. "You gotta love this place, but next year we're renting a sound system that doesn't suck. All right, kids."

As Bell wove off through the partiers, Ebenezer followed at a distance—not close enough to smell the lively clove and peppermint oils woven through her hair but not far enough away to lose sight of her bobbing black tophat or the circle of her hips. The part of her that longed to hear the toast was just as tall, wide, and deadly as the part that did not, and both were currently engaged in a great civil war.

The microphone shrieked as he adjusted it, and the Baby Jesus raised his arms in benediction.

"Yeah, I get that a lot, for some reason." The jibe got more than a hearty laugh. "So, she said she'd do a toast, because you all insisted."

Bell bopped him on the halo with the mic.

138

"Yeah, you'd think I liked talking or something. What, I take my clothes off and roll around in raspberry preserves once, and suddenly I'm a toastmaster?" She flipped her wrist demurely as the partiers applauded. "Anyway, I'll keep this short so we can all get started dancing, or get back to posing like statues, or whatever pretentious crap we're doing next.

"I can't have these things without awesome friends, so thank you all for coming and being awesome. But there's a lot of awesome people who couldn't make it. So, if you'd raise a glass, a ginger ale bottle, or just your hand to them?" She demonstrated, and all hands obeyed.

"To absent friends—Ash, Tamara, Luz Violetta, may their Vermont poly-household be more fabulous than this mess."

Laughter rolled through the audience like thunder.

"And Yuri, Tim, Cho, and Marley who, apparently, had better things to do than me."

More snickers; Ebenezer rolled her eyes.

Bell's smile flattened. "But, seriously, kids. I want to dedicate this evening mostly to my favorite actress, who…well, isn't really having fun tonight, as many of you know. So," she raised her hand, fingers curving like a glass. "To absent friends—and particularly Ebenezer."

The gesture rippled through the gathering with a robotic stiffness that told Ebenezer everything. Leaning against one of the boxing ring's foam supports, Green scoffed so loud heads turned. She crossed her arms and frowned so brutally Ebenezer backed away. Abruptly, she remembered a name—Jill. Sharp and ugly, like its bearer. No less hateful than she had been in college.

"Jesus, kid. What did you do, kill her dog?" New York City said at her shoulder. The genius had acquired a toga, a clown nose, and a necklace made from bottle caps, and she was reeling slightly as if drunk. "Got it outside," she explained proudly. "Lobster girl had some." Merry gunfire broke out across her shoulders, and she giggled.

Ebenezer's arms crossed, too.

"It's not your business. We just had a very public fight at one of Bell's stupid things, and Marley found it unacceptable."

"Because if you did kill her dog, you should know the seventh floor of Brooksfield Apartments thanks you."

"She knew I hadn't had a role in years," Ebenezer shouted. "And she had to just wave her part in *Wicked* in my face right after Marley told me to send out head shots again or get on with my life.

"We fought all the way over in the cab. She just wouldn't shut the fuck up about it. So, when Jill pranced up like she always did in school, I had enough. Drinks got thrown. I may have used the words *bitch-faced syphilis sore*. Marley dragged me home and left for the night. I punched pillows and drank a lot."

New York City whistled. "Yeah, I'd forgotten that. Good times. Hey, don't gimme that look. I see and hear all, remember? Speaking of seeing, look over there." The genius leaned on Ebenezer's shoulder and turned her around.

"Wanna tell me what *that* was?"

Bell was no more than five inches away, and Ebenezer could not back up. Jill stood behind her, and the two conversed through her as if she were an open window. The genius tugged her hand like a string, and Ebenezer sidled from the sandwich.

Jill's green nails tap-tap-tapped her bony elbows.

"I sighed. So what?"

"Yeah, except your average sigh can't be heard in the Bronx."

Until now, Ebenezer had not been aware that Bell's body understood anger—understood it truly, as a function of sinew and blood not the puppeting of flesh for an audience.

Jill's fingers fluttered like finch wings.

"Look, Bell, I don't like saying this—"

"Coulda fooled me. You forget, your little throwdown happened at my Not-Valentine's Day Party."

"It's more than parties. If anybody's happy, or has anything, she ruins it. That's what crazy people do. She can't *not* act like a freak and an asshole, even when she had Marley."

"Well, I will give you that—her not having Marley's a big problem. Though clearly not for the same reason you think." Bell took one step closer. "It's the holidays, Jill."

The flapper brushed Bell's hand away.

"We get it. You like projects. You like challenges. But Andy learned not to be a creepy jerk, and Mariam's got some weird bone disease. What's her excuse?" She stepped back as Bell stepped closer, fists clenched like hams at her sides. "Bell, look. You wonder why everybody came this time? Even me and that other girl she yelled at?"

"Well, here I thought it was because I threw good parties. Who knew?" One fist uncurled on the blonde's slim shoulder. "Your objection's duly noted. But I think you need to go now. You can go home with Collette or not. Whatever she wants to do." Bell turned away without goodbye and strode off shouting, "Dreidle time! I'm dealing!"

Ebenezer stared after Bell's retreating hips, completely unaware how wide her mouth had opened, or how full her eyes were.

New York City had snatched a bright red apple from a passing Gothic Lolita's plate. Extracting a knife from her left scapula, she delicately began to peel it.

"I don't get you, Ebenezer. She likes her friends; she's made a job doing two things she loves in the shittiest economy even I can remember; she clearly brushes her teeth, and she's one of the five genuinely happy people in my borders who can say they're genuinely happy with a straight face. And God knows why, but she seems to like you." She bit into a slice and chewed, following Ebenezer's gaze. "Not that hard on the eyes, either."

"That's not it," Ebenezer said, so softly even she had trouble hearing.

"Well, then what's wrong with her? Sure, Jill's a bitch—well, more than you, anyway— but everyone has a shitty friend."

"No. Not that," Ebenezer watched as Bell bounced the *Star Trek* baby on one great thigh. "She wants to be my friend."

The genius got that thoughtful look that heralded some wise saw or another, but Red Flapper pushed between the pair like a gunshot.

"Jill? Baby, what happened?"

"Clearly we can't blaspheme the name of Saint Ebenezer in her holy presence." Jill looped an arm around Red's waist.

"Oh, yes. Nobody must ever call Bell on her shit," Red kissed her cheek. "I really just don't get her tastes. Or Marley's."

"I don't like her new guy, either," Red agreed. "Nikolai's cuter and nicer. His brother's just so…quiet."

"But Yuri wasn't taken," Jill reminded her. "Let's go. Sick of this fucking cult-like party."

Ebenezer did not watch them leave. She was too busy wondering how she could still breathe.

Yuri Biryukov.

The smell of sound booth and theatre threatened to overpower her.

"Kid?" New York City shook her gently.

Ebenezer lacked the will to shrug away from the great blinking hand.

"You knew."

"I won't deny that, no."

The room felt too bright, and too slow. There were far too many people dancing. Smiles that cut. Laughter like blows. Ebenezer felt each vertebrae lock as her head turned. She wanted to ask why, but the question seemed just as trite as any explanation the genius could give. Instead, she spoke up from her gut, and without thinking at all.

"Take me to Marley."

Scene VII

Release

The snow whipped her face, and the wind had tugged her ponytail loose some time ago; Ebenezer noticed no more than she cared.

She was walking through the Village streets with no thought for direction, or anything but Marley's freckled thighs, her pert breasts, her lips, her red hair like a wound against the sky.

His hands with their flat palms, his wide shoulders. His laugh, like buckshot.

She remembered Yuri now. He had Nikolai's smile but not his heat—there was always something sub-zero about sound designers. The sound booths, chilly to protect the equipment. Overkill even in summer.

The blue flicker of an Xbox across his face. Was that the system he had rigged in the little theater in Harlem Marley had dragged her to last year? Had she knocked on the booth door and called his name, and had he answered, or was this all fancy? Had they smiled at each other when she wasn't looking?

His name over dinner ("Such wonderful sound-scapes, Ebbie!"). His quiet presence at two of Bell's

144

parties, where he had whiled away the evening by the table, talking up the finer points of Polish cuisine to Marley's ever-blooming smile.

Had they met up during the long tech rehearsals while Ebenezer stirred her Cup-O-Noodles and waited, and wanted? When had it happened? While her kisses grew more desperate, and Marley's silences longer and fiercer even than their arguing? Had she seen it far away like a locomotive, yet stood and made no move?

Ebenezer could have torn herself to pieces.

"Take me to Marley!"

She had clawed at New York City's robes and arms, and still the genius had looked down with her eyes deep as the Hudson and said no. So, there had been nothing else but to run stumbling along like a drunkard, like a woman shackled.

If the genius would not listen, *she* would find her. If it took tearing down Manhattan brick by brick, scaffold by scaffold, she'd find her.

How did Yuri touch her? Did he enjoy the slope of her nose and the beauty mole on her right breast?

Did she still cry?

"Hey! Wait up!"

The voice came as if shouted through the Lincoln Tunnel. It reminded her of ghosts, and she pressed on.

The street was so very full of memory. Marley leaning against a lamppost, circumscribed by an aureole of amber. Marley snuggled in a diner booth, her nose leaky and fever-red. Marley peeking from a passing cab. Marley in each window, each doorway, each shuttered storefront. A million Marleys, twenty million, falling down on her like night and all its missiles. From every crack and every corner she besieged her, every fight and disagreement, every harsh word and harsher silence.

Well, Ebbie. I don't know what to say, except you'll never be a famous actress if you sit there feeling sorry for yourself.

Why don't you talk to me?

You know what your problem is? You want all of these things, but you never try.

Each memory struck Ebenezer like a fist. Shivering from a greater cold within, she raised her hands against the weather to force them back.

"No," she begged. "Please. No more. I can't."

But the ghosts enclosed her, merged into the sentence Marley had driven through her world like a coffin nail. She covered her ears, trembled, shouted, yet it shot through her skull again, like blood, like the splitting of teak wood.

Like an iron chain yanked across concrete.

I'm sorry. I can't do it anymore.

A hand was on her arm.

"No," Ebenezer pleaded. "No, don't touch me."

It would not let her pull away.

Marley was dead, and the city was haunted by her.

"Kid? Hey, kid!"

New York City's voice, foghorn-clear, concerned. Ebenezer's head shot up against her will, each vertebrae cracking like a separate link.

The genius held her lit torch high, and its warmth circled the actress in a kind of spotlight. Squinting,

Ebenezer thought she could almost see the city's face; for the first time since their meeting, concern had flat-lined her lips.

"Are you okay?"

"Oh, God," Ebenezer brought a hand to her mouth and bit the knuckles. She could not crumple now, she told herself. Not with Marley so close—the real Marley, not these shadows. She had to calm down, to take deep breaths, Alexander breaths, yoga breaths.

Rage shot out like a bullet nonetheless.

"You knew. Goddamnit, you knew!"

She was stomping, flailing like a child.

If her outburst offended the city, for once, she made no comment.

"I know everything that goes on in me, remember? Settle down. Please."

Ebenezer's mind spun through a thousand foul things to call the genius. Each of them died on her lips at that "please."

"Why?" she asked instead.

New York City sighed. Suddenly, her lights dimmed, as if someone had flipped them over to grayscale.

"Because you don't get what you want when you want it," she said with a gentleness that made Ebenezer hate her more. "You're a big girl. It's not a new story. Look," she continued when the actress's glare did not let up. "The reason you're a pain—you want to know? You don't think about anyone but yourself."

"As if you do!" Ebenezer shouted. Her skull felt too tight, entirely too hot. "You're the most selfish, fuck-ing cruel and lonely and depressing city in the world."

"If that makes you feel better."

Ebenezer could not remember having ever been so tired, as if the chains she imagined dangling from her wrists and neck had themselves sprouted chains.

"I'm done here. I'm done. I'll find her without your help."

She did not expect the genius to call her back after just five steps.

"All right. Obviously, you may not like what you see."

"I'll manage." Ebenezer snarled

"Yep. You're just great at that. Grow up, Ebenezer. Just grow up." The city's yellow eyes rolled with impatience, but her voice lacked its usual granite. "You don't have to be fourteen anymore."

Then, why does it hurt so much? she didn't bother asking.

"Come here," New York City said, and held her arms wide, like a benediction.

And Ebenezer entered them like a worshipper.

As a teenager, looking out on winter and bare cottonwoods, she had imagined New York City as a much kinder place—not full of concrete walls and these steel shadows cold and sharp as a knife drawer. The genius's embrace was like a subway wind and the thrum of radiators—warm and electrical, vaguely dusty. It was not kind, but neither was it unkind; her pulsing arms were Broadway and adrenaline, her body a million lights beneath its drape.

One seemed to be getting brighter—and then closer, as if stretching up to meet her. Ebenezer felt her limbs stretching as well. At first, the sensation was pleasant, like a long stretch before breakfast; but gradually, her muscles pulled and her joints cracked warningly. Her arms were pulled up as if drawn by a magnet; the rest of her followed into the yellow light on New York City's shoulder.

The wind kicked through her snarled hair, and snow stung her face like pins. Blinking through the prickles, Ebenezer no longer saw the genius's robe but only sky swirled red with snow and neon. Lacquered in white, the buildings beneath her fluttering coat reminded her of despoiled ossuaries.

She was going down too fast. Too fast.

"Later, kid. Good luck. I guess."

The words seemed to well from sky and street and roof. Then, New York City spoke no more save only as air and the knockabout of traffic.

As she drifted down like in a bad dream, Ebenezer recognized the streets of Spanish Harlem. A gable straightened from its slouch, reaching out for her...

Scene VIII

Incessant Torture
of Remorse

Ebenezer plummeted through decades of tar and pitch, creaky supports, and people in all stages of sleep and congress. Nine floors down, she crashed through a kitchen's ghastly floral linoleum and onto the mangy carpet in the room beneath. The impact's force rippled up her arms and through her kneecaps, briefly reminding her of her age.

The apartment was shabby but meticulously clean, and filled with racks of CDs, speakers, subwoofers and all manner of musical instruments. Drums stood at the posts of the black-sheeted bed like sentries, and a keyboard perched atop a sleek black armoire, legs up suggestively. Ebenezer felt her heart clench like a fist; the apartment was even smaller than her own.

Yet it appeared to be empty. Where was Marley? Was this just some random location? It was definitely something New York City would do.

A quarter-turn, however, revealed a kitchen tucked beneath a loft, and Marley leaning against the countertop, a glass of red wine dangling from one hand, her ginger hair bound back and swept down to the right in a soft coil. Her cheeks matched her dress, which was far too scarlet and satiny for staying in, and her freckles stood out against her blush as if painted on. Her eyes were moist, for reasons Ebenezer hoped she'd guessed correctly.

"Marley," she said, not able to think of anything that sounded better.

Marley took a gulp of wine instead of answering. A pot of something green simmered on the range top to her right, and handfuls of battered onions crackled in a well-greased frying pan.

Ebenezer's anger crackled, too.

"Don't ignore me. Don't you dare."

A toilet flushed, and both women's heads turned towards a narrow passage running parallel to the little kitchen. A door near its end opened, and a dun-haired man emerged.

His clothes were as black as the bed sheets—a pair of respectably worn jeans and a T-shirt for some band Ebenezer didn't recognize. He had Nikolai's rounded jaw and his broad cheeks but not the handsome dark curls or the dancer's build. Rather, he was at least 250 pounds—too much even for a frame that boasted ten inches on her own height, and most of it far from muscle.

"Sorry about that."

Yuri passed her by without a glance. Ebenezer felt like tripping him. Instead, she watched as he reached into an open cabinet and took down a box of chocolates. A glance at the contents was all the explanation she required for his girth. So did the plate of veggie burgers and another filled with the pierogis folded on the counter.

Ebenezer's temperature climbed even further. Were they eating together now?

"Hey," he said, gently tapping the box against Marley's bare arm.

She turned and offered him the small half-smile she always made when sad.

"Hey," she replied as she selected one dark nougat. She sighed and then forgot to bite it.

"That bad, huh?"

"That bad."

Yuri went about selecting several sweets.

"You know, chocolate is very good for that. For most things. So I hear, anyway. Especially if it's German."

This earned a chuckle as Marley finally popped the neglected sweet into her mouth. The familiar sight of her rounded front teeth and their lipstick stains made Ebenezer hurt.

As she chewed, Marley reached for the glass of wine, only to find Yuri's hand covering the rim.

"Two-glass rule." He said it like a reminder. "Until two months after breaking up. At least." When Marley's shoulders hunched and sagged, he moved a little closer. "You can talk about it. I'm a man, but I promise to listen. As well as I can, of course."

Marley's green eyes suddenly were even brighter.

"It's nothing," she insisted as she reached for a rack of paper towels. "Breakups just suck. Even when you start them. Probably especially then." She dabbed her eyes, and three-fourths of her mascara came away. "Fuck. Sorry. I'm sorry. Never talk about an ex. Ten years, and I forget all the rules." She wiped again, re-peating "Fuck."

Yuri shook his head.

"Rules like that are made by television writers and other monsters. If you want to praise her, praise her. If you want to trash her, trash her."

"And if I'm not even sure I should be doing this, or even be here?" The tissue crumpled in her hand. "Fuck. I don't know."

"Well, then, I will call a cab and walk you down-stairs. And if you call tomorrow asking for space, I will say fine. But I'll still think you shouldn't be alone. That it's not good right now."

This time her laugh was bitter.

"And who else would I call? Everybody telling me good riddance? How I should have done it sooner, be-cause she's crazy, or toxic, or just a raving bitch?" The towel came up again. "You know, I think I'd rather they took her side. Yelled at me. Go back, what the hell were you thinking, Marley? Something. I don't know. I'd rather be the bitch here. It feels fair."

She turned to Yuri, that painful, plaintive look on her face that long ago could make Ebenezer surren-der.

"Just one more glass?"

"It won't help. Trust someone who knows." He cupped her shoulder with a great hand then withdrew it guiltily, a thief caught in the apple cart. "It's been a rough week," he continued in those cottony tones that had always seemed to Ebenezer like an invitation to ignore him.

She felt her teeth grind like millstones as the sound designer led her ex-girlfriend into the living room, to a sofa upholstered in serviceable black velour and a coffee table marked by three mug rings. Neither noticed her as Marley settled her tulip-petal skirts on the cushions.

"There." Yuri placed a mug of something steaming in her hands that smelled faintly of honey and blackberries. "*Sbiten*. Like the mead Bell got Mariam to brew, but better for winter."

Marley acknowledged his estimation with a hum as she took a sip. She smacked her lips and pronounced it good, and Yuri smiled—a shy and small thing at odds with his height and girth.

"It goes best with *pelmeni*," he insisted. "And cabbage soup, and veggie burgers—not the store-brand, either." As if realizing he had somehow derailed himself, he coughed. "But I did not finish the soup on time. Let me put on something while you wait." In two steps he was thumbing through a CD shelf. "There's a lot—if you have any requests?"

"Diana Krall," both women said simultaneously.

"If you've got *The Look of Love*," Marley added.

In the whole room, only Yuri did not flinch.

"A good choice."

His fingers located the jewel case and slipped the disk into a stereo as sturdy as the rest of his possessions. As the opening violins lulled Marley to distraction, he retreated to the kitchen and busied himself stirring the butter-browned onions into a large pot emitting a vaguely green odor.

Until then, Ebenezer was unaware she had not exhaled for at least a minute.

Finally, they were alone. The cushions dipped as she lowered herself beside Marley, who now stared into the depths of her mug as if scrying. She smelled like roses, night, and something uniquely Marley, and Ebenezer breathed her in, not knowing what to say. The words stopped in her throat.

"Why are you doing this to me?" she tried at last.

Marley continued staring into her mug, one long finger circling its rim, perhaps in search of answers. It angered Ebenezer.

"Look at me," she snapped.

Marley stared.

"Five minutes," Yuri informed through the steam and bubbles.

"All right." Marley turned her head and looked right through Ebenezer.

Right through her.

Ebenezer's veins iced ip. It was New York City's last and greatest fuck-over; in Marley's view, she was truly part of the furniture, in more than one way.

"Looks good," her ex-girlfriend noted.

"I have made it vegetarian. Just for you."

Ebenezer suddenly wanted to punch that big, stupid smile.

"She isn't yours!" she shouted at him, leaping up so fast the sofa bumped. She could not understand how Marley didn't feel it, or how the interloper couldn't see the lightning she wanted to aim for his heart.

He didn't hear her, either.

"But just vegetarian. The *pelmeni* have *quark*—it's a cream cheese. Really soft. I'm sorry, I wasn't think—"

Setting down her mug, Marley stood and crossed the room.

"It's okay." Standing on her tiptoes, she draped her thin arms over his shoulders. "They'll be lovely. Like always."

As Ebenezer watched, lump in her throat, Marley pecked a kiss against his stubble then leaned in to kiss more. But halfway there, she retreated and turned her face away, her blush so bright her skin might well have been a beacon.

"Sorry. I shouldn't have. It's…"

"Too soon," Yuri concluded sympathetically.

Marley interlaced her fingers and shuffled back a few steps. Her next words struggled out as if through wet soil.

"I like you a lot. I really do. I don't want to be wishy-washy, or to lead you on. But I *am* wishy-washy—or maybe just confused." She chuckled without mirth. "What a shitty, bratty, girly thing to say, huh?"

"There's nothing about you that is shitty or bratty," Yuri insisted. "Girly, though…"

Marley's smile wavered down into a grimace, then back into splotchy tears.

"I really loved her. But she just…I don't know if she was too sick or angry to admit there was a problem or just as scared as I was about it. A lot of problems, really."

"Me, right?"

She laughed bitterly.

"No. That would have meant she was paying attention for once. I don't even think she noticed you, except maybe as some kind of fucked-up competition for professional recognition or whatever else she believed was actually important in life."

"Except I did notice," Ebenezer said coldly. By now, she did not really expect an answer.

Her ex wiped her eyes on her knuckles.

"I don't know what those things actually were, of course. It sucks when one partner's more successful. Of course it does. But it was more. She'd never just— it was like a guessing game. 'Tell me why I'm mad or else you don't care.' Like throwing a tantrum was easier than talking.

"She's been miserable since we met, but not like how she got in the last year or so. Every day, nothing was right, but when I'd ask she'd just throw up her hands…" Marley demonstrated, "…and sigh. She was just *there*, without any map to show how to reach her, or an answer key. I'd just give up trying."

"She had a lot of disappointments." Yuri's tone was far more clinical than Ebenezer liked.

Marley's laugh was like a bark—the kind of laugh she always gave when she was angry.

"And she never stops telling anyone who will listen all about them. She did most of them to herself, so she's an expert." She wiped her eyes again. "Fuck. You know what's the worst thing? I didn't want to leave. Even when I worked out what I felt for you, that just made it worse.

"I mean, you're wonderful—anyone who would not say that is stupid. But if you're happy with someone—someone you're dating—you don't notice. At least, you're not supposed to, if everything's going okay.

"But I thought, 'What would it be like to come home and just once not have to deal with all that drama and impossibleness? Just once.' And it was like I found a map, and a key to the door."

The pot lid rattled, interrupting them.

"It's ready. Sorry. Please keep talking."

157

"I don't know what else there is to say." Marley paced back to his side as he fiddled with the stove's gleaming knobs. "I'm miserable for Christmas. Now that she actually wants to talk, I won't. So, she feels worse and is probably doing something stupid…" Trembling a little, Marley clutched a fist to her breastbone, ending that thought right there. "And all of it's not fair to you."

Yuri shook his head as he fetched a ladle from a black holder embossed with silver quarter-notes.

"Why don't you let me be the judge of that?"

"It isn't! Because I'm clearly not over her, which is really shitty of me, no matter what you say. And I'm angry at her, and sad, and being immature about it, too, and we don't need any more drama. We get enough of that at work." Her fingers found the fall of red hair and tugged it sharply. "It's not right to be your girlfriend if I keep thinking every day about going back, saying I'm sorry, and getting our asses into counseling."

"Is that what you want?"

Marley lowered her eyes and did not speak for a very, very long time.

"At first I thought it was, but after the third day—all that weight was gone, and even though I felt like the biggest asshole ever, I knew it was the right choice. It's better for her if I move on, or so I keep telling myself. And it's better for me, too. Because you'd make a great boyfriend."

Yuri swilled the ladle through the cabbage soup.

"I see. That is what you want from me?"

Marley's hand slipped on top of his.

"Things are just…really, really bad right now, but they're not wrong. It's like growing pains, I guess. That's a really long way of saying yes. I hope so. Soon."

158

This time she did not pull out of the kiss.

The ice that had filled Ebenezer's veins shattered. She burst through the door like mist before she knew what she had done. The hallways and staircases turned and plunged like an Escher lithograph. Her stomach pitched and yawed along with them; twice she slammed into a wall and vomited the food she had so recently consumed. The passages felt too close, too small and strange, and the perspiration underneath her arms felt like sleet. Twice she fell, banging up one knee and skinning both palms.

I drove her away! Her mind screamed like a siren. *I drove her away!*

She had no idea how she found the first floor, or the door leading out into the street, except her hand closed on the handle and she was through, bruising her other knee as she stumbled down the stairs into the street below.

As shock coursed through what felt like every cell in her system, Ebenezer dug the heels of her palms into her eyes. Salt mingled with the metal scent of blood, and both stung; she hardly noticed.

"I drove her away."

Her chest felt like it was breaking. So did the sky. And it was all true. At twenty-nine, she had failed in all things, and somehow this one hurt the most. She had never felt so punctured; the tears and sobs and screams poured out like a flood.

"I've ruined everything," she concluded. "Everything. There's nothing else. Nothing. And she still loves me. It could have worked."

That seemed to be the end of it; not for the first time in her life, Ebenezer wished for death.

There was a sound like rustling leaves, and creeping sand.

ACT IV

The Last of the
Spirits

Scene I

Uncertain Horror

Vaguely, Ebenezer noticed the street was darkening, but she did not care to determine why or even to look up. Her tears were overwhelming, and the heaviness upon her limbs felt more like chains than ever.

As she hugged herself, splayed out where she had fallen in the snow like the piniored figure of the Ten of Swords, she wondered, as clichéd as the notion was, if her heart had shattered like glass. It felt that way.

Then something jerked her body up onto its knees, as if pulling it by a string. It was just enough to jar her from a sob.

The street was dark and empty as a snuffed fire-place. Even the sky had been drained of its red snow-storm cast, and now looked like a corpse three hours dead. Puzzlement edged out the breaking feeling in her chest, and Ebenezer let the tears cool on her cheeks.

It seemed as though she had crossed back into her own private city, only something was very wrong. The snow had stopped, which made the street more deso-late, but that wasn't it entirely.

The very air was broken, as if something had torn open that should have remained sealed at any cost.

163

A breeze picked up, dry and thin, as if it came through bare elm branches—or rattling lungs.

Grief is potent, but terror can unseat it with a glance. The invisible cord jerked again; Ebenezer stumbled to her feet, banged knees screaming, raw palms stunned in the rush of air.

Something was moving in the gloom.

At first, she thought it was a moonbeam's trick, but the moon was nowhere to be seen in a sky now low and fog-choked. Although, even in the darkness, she could tell something was approaching fast, and that it was strangely visible.

She squinted until her eyes stung with the effort and the vestiges of tear-salt. It was like looking at a rush of wind without leaves or swirling trash to mark its progress. Like looking at a rip of night, or going blind in just one place. Whatever it was, it filled Ebenezer with a cold and sweatless horror, and she could not look away.

The apparition—for she could think of no better term—closed in like a curtain, and the temperature fell with it. When it stopped just feet from her, Ebenezer could hear as well as feel her teeth chattering, and the numbness of her skin. This close, the pain of looking at it receded just enough for her straining eyes to focus.

As far as she could tell, the thing was vaguely woman-shaped, on the small and slender side with tangled hair, and its…her…body was not entirely void. If she squinted her dry and aching eyes, Ebenezer could almost make out forms—the eyeless windows of great skyscrapers, the roads of unknown cities, a round face framed by jags of magenta hair. It was like view-

164

ing a film running on a shattered projector through a veil of moving water.

The figure raised an impossible arm and uncurled what must have been a fist. Ebenezer's eyes stung again as white light seared her retinas even after she brought her eyelids down. When the spots had danced away, she cracked one lid carefully until she could see again.

A small hourglass perched in that watermark of a palm, shining like a white flame. It appeared to be made of bone and glass, its sand little specks of light that tumbled grain by grain, so slowly they almost stood still. A sound very much like wind filled her ears—no, not wind, for it had a tidal pulse.

Was the hourglass *breathing*? Ebenezer gulped.

"What are you?" she asked, her voice sounding high and young.

The figure said nothing, but Ebenezer thought she saw its head—or what passed for it—tilt in her direction. The answer flashed like a light bulb blowing, like memory recalled, as though she had thought of it herself.

"The Genius of the Future."

It sounded strange when spoken aloud—for how, she thought, could things yet to be have borders, or people, as Utah and New York City had?

Oh, New York City and Utah. Ebenezer knew she would have traded anything to glimpse Utah's motherly smile, to see New York City peeking from the apparition's hood, laughing like a fool and insisting it was all a well-deserved prank for one sin or another.

The Future knows all lands and all outcomes. These are its road signs and its traffic lights. The Kingdom of

165

Possibility exists just beyond a blink, shadowed barely. It can, therefore, be called No Thing and No Place, and Every Thing and Every Place at once. No more questions now.

"But," she tried, "but—why are you here? If the Future is blank, how can I see you? How can I—what do you want?"

The genius did not move at all, yet Ebenezer knew it was laughing at her. Her rage burned like a pilot light, unable to fully ignite.

Fingers closed on hers. Cold branched through her body like a fractal, freezing her scream as the world blew a fuse. She had a sensation of falling, as though entering the earth, spinning deep into its womb. Her body seemed to shake into its several parts—stomach here, brain there, a mess of veins and arteries fanning out like anemone. Had she been able to locate her mouth and stomach, Ebenezer knew she would have vomited a third time that night.

Then, just when she thought she would dissipate into a billion grains of sand, the world smacked down and her body jarred back together. Falling to her knees like a dropped marionette, her prediction half came true—will alone managed to keep down the remains of the international meal she had consumed what felt like a universe away now.

Perhaps it was.

When she felt well enough to move, she slowly opened her eyes and gasped.

She was sitting in the middle of the cubicle farm.

Scene II

To Profit Us
When Dead

Ebenezer scrambled to her feet just in time to avoid a pair of red knife-blade high heels. The woman wearing them was Cynthia, who, as usual, strode across the dark-gray carpet without regard for anything in her path or in her wake.

"Carker and Tulkinghorn," Ebenezer observed. She leaned against one partition to get her bearings. "You brought me to work."

She turned to the genius and immediately felt sick again. Even though the high fluorescents buzzed and the granite cast of a New York City winter morning seeped through the windows, the figure was as lightless and vague as ever. And just as silent.

"Well, why?"

The inside of her head buzzed only with her own thoughts.

"Look," she tried, "I don't know what you are, exactly. How you do things where…wherever it is you come from. But I can't just magically know what I'm doing here, or what it is you want me to see." Her passivity bothered her, but not nearly as much as the genius's lack of response.

"Just tell me what to do. Please?"

The Future holds no instructions, Ebenezer.

The genius stared at her. She stared back. And felt her anger bubble to the surface once again.

"Well, fuck you," she snapped, and turning so fast she stumbled, she marched off after Cynthia's swooshing slacks. "Goddamned spirits," she muttered as an afterthought, to make herself feel braver.

As Cynthia's strawberry-blond curls disappeared around a corner, Ebenezer realized she had just passed her cubicle. Curiosity seized her and shook her hard. Based on all the bad sci-fi movies she and Marley had watched, would her current self be able to withstand the sight of her future self without losing her mind or watching the universe implode?

Oh, Marley...

Ebenezer shook her head to banish the thoughts of long red hair and couch sex after movie night. Really, when it came to the possibility of all known things combusting or remembering anything about Marley, Ebenezer knew what her choice would always be.

So she turned to find her work station occupied, but not by her. That is, unless the future held a transformation into a balding white man who looked two beats away from cardiac arrest, and whose screaming put him even closer to total heart death. Both Left and Right peeked over their walls to see what the fuss was all about—and whether, perhaps, they should call security.

"If you don't pay now, bitch, I will be at your house in thirty minutes! Jail isn't very fucking nice to bitches like you sitting around on your fat asses and taking money from honest working people." He listened for a moment. "Get an education, ma'am. Your diabetes is all your fault for being stupid and buying Twinkies with other people's money. I hope you lose your feet. I hope you get—"

The caller must have hung up, because he swore and slammed the phone into its cradle.

"Wow," Ebenezer whispered. "Did I really sound like that?"

Seeing as she was not the thin man now gritting his teeth and bringing up another number to harass, she decided that she did—too frequently.

And then, another realization.

"In the future, I get fired." She slapped her hands onto her thighs. "Great! Just great."

She looked over her shoulder to find the Genius of the Future. She was standing next to the water cooler, looking vacantly ahead as Trent filled a Dixie cup. Why he and the entire farm were not stumbling around in panic, uprooting tables at the presence of this thing— for she could not quite think of her as a woman—Ebenezer could not fathom. Was the future every bit as unremarkable as any other place?

"Hey," she hissed. "Hey—what the hell? You bring me here to show me that I'm now out of work and probably out on the streets? What the hell?" It was the only thing that sounded right, so Ebenezer repeated it a third time.

The genius did not acknowledge her. The living hourglass in her hand dropped a grain, and Ebenezer failed to suppress a shudder. The object stirred more dread and sickness in her than its holder did. What it was, she could not fathom, except its breathing carried over the cubicle farm's bustle like the whisper of an air conditioner.

Trent crushed his cup into the trash can, turned, and took Cynthia's path along the rows. As he passed her, Ebenezer stepped after him. Perhaps, she told herself, he was going to her office. Perhaps there was some paperwork—or something—there, detailing when and why she had been let go.

Although she suspected the fault lay in her numbers, she had no better ideas. At least, she reasoned, she could figure out what day it was, what year, so when she managed to escape this nightmare, or whatever it was exactly, she would know how long she had to hunker down and prepare.

Instead of turning left, Trent rounded the corner Cynthia had taken, passed another bank of unidentifiable employees, and opened the door to Fred's office. Her lip between her incisors, Ebenezer followed him inside and discovered Cynthia standing placidly in front of a cluttered but still functional desk. Fred sat behind it, and Ebenezer was thankful that none of them appeared to hear her sharp intake of breath— or care if they had heard it.

"My God," she whispered. "What happened to you, Fred?"

Her supervisor had looked no different at first—his white shirt was still uncreased, his tie an appropriate shade of red and knotted firmly at his starched collar. But he looked like his shadow, slow in motion, faded. His smile was gone. This frightened Ebenezer most of all.

The door shut behind Trent with a crisp little click.

"All right," he said, clapping his hands in that over-friendly way that meant he was just about to rip out a throat. "Everybody's here? Then let's get started."

Apparently, that was Cynthia's cue to turn on the pre-programmed, oozy sympathy.

"Fred, we understand you're taking recent events very hard—"

"A member of my team is dead, Ms. Sheldon."

Something cold crawled through Ebenezer's stomach. *He didn't say who*, she reminded herself. *Maybe I'm just fired*.

Cynthia sucked in a startled breath. "Well…"

"Of course. It's terrible," Trent said brusquely. "A terrible shock to all of us. But these things happen. All the time."

Fred's face twisted.

"And that means it's no big deal," he said in a very un-Fred-like way.

Trent didn't miss a beat.

"No one is saying that, Fred. But life has to go on, and it just doesn't seem to be doing that for you. You haven't been on time all month. You leave early. The rest of your team—who are very much alive, remember—say they bring you their concerns, but you don't listen and don't act."

"As if he'd ever do that," Ebenezer muttered. The cold feeling hadn't left, though.

"I asked for a few weeks off," Fred reminded them, sounding tired.

"During one of our busiest months," Cynthia reminded him, like clockwork. "It was not a good time for a breakdown, Fred."

Fred said nothing. He just looked at them.

Trent tapped his fingertips together thoughtfully, looking all the more menacing to Ebenezer for his lack of menace.

"We both think," he said at last, "your priorities may be changing."

"Oh, like hell." Ebenezer's rage surprised her. It was a feeling usually reserved for herself.

"They're just what they always were," Fred said without his usual congeniality.

"That's not the sense we've gotten," Trent said.

"I was late the day after…after it happened and on the twenty-fourth," Fred reminded them, sounding even more washed out. "My punch cards should show that."

"You've been distant. Disengaged," Cynthia continued, as if he hadn't spoken.

Fred sucked his lower lip, clearly fighting back a sigh—or perhaps it was a scream. This worn-down Fred, Ebenezer realized, was likely capable of both.

"You said no time off. I agreed that was fine. So I've been here every day, doing my best. Like everybody here."

"We just think you need to reevaluate your priorities," Trent said. "And whatever you decide, whatever you want to do about your work here, we'll respect that."

Fred looked like he had something to say. However, after several seconds of Trent and Cynthia's corporate smiles, he sighed.

"It's good we're on the same page," Cynthia said.

And that was that. The two left with a "we appreciate your thoughts" but without a backward glance, not even bothering to shut the door behind them.

Fred obliged instead. The tears beat him back to his desk.

"God." He bowed his face into his large hands. "Oh, my God."

His shoulders shook. The chair shook. He did not look up, even when his sobs became thick with phlegm.

Ebenezer shifted her weight uncomfortably. She hated tears, her own and anybody's, and tonight—or whatever span of time had elapsed since she'd awakened in her lonesome apartment—had been far too full of them.

But watching Fred rock himself through sobs—and all for someone he hardly even knew—seemed...

No. Not seemed. It *was* wrong. Very wrong.

"Hey."

He did not look up as she crossed the room, but Ebenezer put her arm around his back anyway, regretting more than anything she could recall the casual discarding of his candy cane gift.

It was not only appropriate to say something, but necessary, she decided.

"You're too good for this job," she tried. "For any of us, including whoever it is you're mourning for. And especially me. I've been...I didn't need to be such an ass to you. I'm sorry."

But of course, she was as invisible as air. Fred only wept harder. She rubbed his broad back, blushing from the unfamiliarity of it all.

"Please, don't cry." She recalled her grandmother saying that whenever her granddaughter fell, whenever her classmates threw sticks and punches at her face, whenever her tears just felt too heavy for her skull.

173

It rarely worked, of course, but it was the best thing she knew.

"Please, Fred. I'm so sorry. I…I'm just so sorry."

The raspy sound of breathing filled the room. Ebenezer looked over her shoulder. The Genius of the Future stood in the corner by the window, the weak-tea sunbeams vanishing entirely in the void of her, across which familiar faces—including what appeared to be Fred's—fell past like magnolia petals.

"I don't understand." Ebenezer told her.

The figure looked on, and suddenly it all made sense.

"Oh, God…" Ebenezer whimpered, staggering away from her still-weeping supervisor. "Oh…"

The replacement: a knife-twist in her stomach.

I worry about her. Fred had said that, too.

"Oh, my God," Ebenezer moaned. And then she screamed it. "I'm dead! I'm dead! I'm dead!"

She repeated and repeated her exclamation as Fred cried on behind her, insensible of anything amiss. She screamed herself to hoarseness, past hoarseness into a quiet, animal trembling. All the while, the genius observed her neutrally, making no attempt at comfort, or even motion. The timepiece in her null hand made a sound like raven's wings and let fall another twinkling grain.

"What happened?" Ebenezer choked out at last. "How did it happen? Why did — Oh, oh, God …"

The genius merely grabbed her hand again, and Ebenezer spun down into darkness.

Scene III

An Empty Chair

A telephone's insistent ringing—Ebenezer heard that long before the painful blackness lifted. When it did, her head felt as if it had been cleaved and haphazardly stuck back together. Again, she was thankful her stomach had nothing more to disgorge—although the carpet beneath her probably would not have minded.

The genius had returned her to the Cratchits' dim apartment, which looked even dirtier than the last time she had entered, however long ago it was. The diffused light suggested winter or a slow spring. But what day, exactly?

The disorienting form of travel the genius insisted upon taking hurt far worse the second time, but Ebenezer found the pain had calmed her and restored some focus. Although time was currently irrelevant, the encounter with Marley was fresh and unscabbed. It hurt, Ebenezer thought, more than a disgusting job, than childhood embarrassment and adult paralysis. More than anything, save for one thing—her stillborn talent.

For what reason did her heart keep beating, without the latter? What purpose did a tortoise shell of a life serve when there was no one waiting at home, no one likely to wait ever again?

Perhaps death was preferable.

The thought both relieved and shamed her as she considered her mother—the slashed wrists and promises, all the disgust and fear that came with them. But then she remembered darkness, water that ran deep and held both fear and fascination

Ebenezer swallowed once. She was no longer so afraid.

The ringer stopped at last, and the silence shook her from her reverie. Something was very wrong. The apartment was somewhat filthier than she recalled, of course, but this was not the problem. Gloom seemed to be scattered among the litter of pizza boxes and unsorted laundry in haphazard piles. The three people within looked more like mannequins posed in a tableau of grief than breathing beings.

Martha's great recliner slouched in front of the television. Empty.

Ebenezer rubbed her aching eyes. Yes, empty, and the family, sans Robert, had arranged themselves as if it were a black hole. Claire and Paul sat subdued on the tattered sofa as the television fed them a generic cartoon, but their eyes looked inward, elsewhere. Florence slouched between them, a valiantly vacant expression silkscreened to her face. It switched to life only when Claire tugged at her shirt.

"Hey, Aunt Flo? When's Dad coming home?"

"Hopefully, any minute now—at least before seven." The quiver in her voice was scant, but Ebenezer heard it nonetheless.

"Why's he have to be so late?" The girl kicked her feet listlessly. "I miss him."

"There's a lot grown-ups have to do when somebody…" She could not say it. "After things like this happen."

"Say it, Aunt Florence."

Aunt and sister turned to Paul, who had sat so quietly throughout the conversation he might as well not have been there at all. Yet, his eyes…

"Say it," he repeated. "Say Mom's dead."

Florence lurched a bit, as if lightning had come too near.

"W–well," she tried. "That's right, you guys. She's not coming back. And you've both got to be strong."

Paul slammed his fists into the cushions.

"She's not coming back! You've got to be strong!" He mimicked. "That's what they always tell us! Stupid things like that."

"Paul, listen, okay? She was my mom, too. I feel just as bad."

"I already had a mom." Tears marshaled in the corners of his eyes, but he bit down on his lip until they retreated. "She left. Everybody always leaves."

Florence brought a hand to her mouth to stop her lips' trembling.

"She didn't want to. She never wanted to leave you. Or us."

"But she did!" Paul flinched away when his aunt reached for his shoulders. "No!"

Florence's own tears came.

"She fought so hard to stay here for everyone. For you. You didn't see. She hung on so hard…her knuckles were so pale—it was like she didn't want to say good-bye. You understand? She loved us all more than anything."

"I don't love her. Or you."

Florence turned a little gray.

"Paul, listen, I know you're angry. I know you don't really mean it. But you can't talk like this now, okay? Dad's really sad, and we have to do so many things this week—"

"He's not my dad! Stop saying that!" The boy was on his feet, his eyes two apocalypses. "I hate you! I hate this whole stupid family!"

"Paul!" his aunt cried as a door slammed hard enough to shake the wall.

She did not, however, move to retrieve him. Instead, she shook and collapsed into her hands.

"God. Oh, God. I hate this. I hate this so much…"

Throughout the row, Claire had huddled on her sofa cushion looking every bit as shaken as her aunt, clearly unsure if she should speak or slide down into the cracks with the dust and loose change. She looked as if she now wore chains upon each of her gangly arms, as if her face had aged without having ever used any of its youthful luster.

With growing horror, Ebenezer studied her brow and saw the first letter spelling out doom. She did not know if the little girl would sit there until she vanished altogether or race after her brother, streaming tears and curses.

Claire did neither. Florence looked up from her palms as the child gracelessly climbed into her lap.

"Brothers are assholes sometimes," she offered.

178

Florence's mouth twitched, but she did not correct or scold. Instead, she took the offered hug.

For the first time in her memory, Ebenezer accepted that she was not very good at observation. Paradoxically, she mused, she understood her weakness now precisely because of what she saw in Claire, and how similar the situation was to her own—a girl waiting up far past her bedtime for news of life or death when she had known little of the first and nothing of the second's depth and breadth.

She understood that cold, black feeling like adrenaline and not the snow that lay over the lawn like a reassuring hand, protecting scraggled lilacs, muddy road, and the prickly fields beyond. She saw and knew the relief only an embrace could give, and knew how long the days would feel for Claire from this moment on.

"Life will snuff her out soon enough," Ebenezer said again. Remorse curled in her stomach. "But I didn't have to have a part in that."

The front doorknob turned, and shrill hinges announced Robert's shuffling in. "Like hell" was the only way to describe the way he looked.

In however many weeks or more that had elapsed since Ebenezer's first encounter with him, Martha's husband had acquired a gravity that could have pulled in planets. The circles underneath his eyes and the hesitation in his steps made his small frame appear even more fragile—like glass strained just a little past its breaking point.

Florence coughed and scrubbed at her eyes as if trying to clean up a crime scene.

"Hey, Dad. Welcome back."

Robert slumped onto the couch in a landslide.

"Hi, ladies. What's up?"

Florence was instantly on her feet.

"I was just asking Claire what we should fix for dinner. My vote was for spaghetti. I brought some home from the restaurant; all we need to do is microwave it." She sounded like a robot.

"We didn't talk about that." This earned Claire a pained look from her aunt.

"Spaghetti's fine," said Robert, already a mile away as his gaze panned the room. "Hey, where's Paul?"

"In you and Mom's bedroom," Claire's tone was surprisingly disdainful for an eight-year-old.

Her father just said, "Oh." When he tried to rise, Florence draped her large hand over his shoulder.

"I think he needs some time."

Claire cursed again, under her breath but not quietly enough to escape Ebenezer. Once again her language went unchecked. Instead, her father made an effort at a smile that Ebenezer found nothing short of afflicting.

"Honey? If I give you five dollars, will you run down to the bodega and get some milk and anything else you want that a dentist might kill me for letting you have?"

"It's okay," Claire said. "You can talk about Mom in front of me. It's Mom."

Robert took one look at her and let his tears fold him in half.

"Oh, Dad. No. No." Putting aside the takeout boxes, Florence joined her family in a hug.

"They want twenty thousand dollars more," Robert explained, flicking the tears from his eyes when they had separated.

Florence gasped, "Why?"

"Hospital stays add up. All the tests. Then there's the consultations, the hidden fees—five hundred bucks for urinalysis!" He sighed as he rubbed his temples. "I don't know what to do with that." He added, almost sotto voce, "The cheapest funeral home I could find wants four thousand."

"That much?" Florence's hands squeezed into fists.

"Right. Even dying isn't free anymore."

"Florence." Robert twitched his head in Claire's direction.

"What does that mean?" the little girl asked, her blue eyes wide.

The telephone interrupted any explanation.

"Jesus Christ!" Florence lunged for it and snatched up the receiver in one fluid motion. "No, we don't have the money," she shouted into it. "No, we don't know when we'll pay you...No, we haven't raised fifty thousand dollars since three-thirty...I don't care if you call the cops, or arrest me, or come down here and beat me up. We don't have it. We don't care. And you are the least of our problems right now. Do not call here again!"

The ancient phone's bell clanged as she dropped the handset into its cradle. Her lip trembled as she faced her family.

"I'm sorry. I'm so sorry you had to hear that. This guy's even worse than that girl was. He just doesn't understand—I'm sorry." She bit her lip and sat down again. "If Belinda hadn't called, and Peter, and everybody else, I'd just unplug it."

A few shuddering breaths and another hug from Claire brought her back.

"Omar said I could get a few more hours with the holiday. He's been great—they all have at work. Maybe they'll have some ideas. A donation jar..."

Robert nodded. "Martha hated charity, but..." He looked at the vacant chair and shrugged.

"I can sell my dolls," Claire piped up. "And my pirate ship." Her face was so firm and grown-up that Ebenezer gasped.

"Oh, honey." It was Florence's turn now to fold her niece in her arms.

"I don't really need them," she insisted, biting down the trembling in her own lip.

"That's really generous of you, sweetie, but we'll be fine." Robert patted her hair, although his expression remained distracted. "We'll be fine."

Ebenezer's mind was filled with the white tiles and starched, scary smell of hospitals as she turned to the genius leaning at her side.

"What's going to happen to them?"

Not expecting an answer, she peered into the spirit's body, searching each fleeting shadow. The hourglass breathed, leaving Ebenezer to fill in the dark spaces between possibilities, each one sadder and bleaker than the next, each one impossible to reject.

"There has to be something," she told the genius, even though such possibilities were even murkier. "Aren't there...places to...?"

"What can I do?" she asked at last.

The figure leaned and grabbed her hand again.

Scene IV

Fellow Travelers
to the Grave

When Ebenezer revived, she was aching on a gray SoHo sidewalk beneath the same gray sky. Rubbing her head to ease the pain and nausea, she raised one eyelid, then the next just as another grain dropped into the hourglass's belly. This was followed by a pinprick raindrop, and another, and another…

With some difficulty, she righted herself and took shelter underneath the overhang of an unfamiliar antique building before she realized the rain had not touched her. Being the weather of the future, she supposed it could not. She did not ask the genius for confirmation, though, or for an update on their location, for at that moment, Bell stepped from the shadows of an alley, arm-in-arm with a familiar man.

"Tim?"

But Ebenezer's surprise was short-lived—sooner or later, the game would be called "Six Degrees of Bellwether."

Somewhere between their last encounter and this undefined future, the businessman's health had apparently improved. His black suit was pressed and his thinning hair gel-stiff beneath an equally smart hat. The color set off his face well; Ebenezer did not fail to notice that it looked healthier now, or that Bell's olive skin looked rather ashy-green. Black had always suited her well, but not this high-collared rayon black or the soft black of her hair bound tightly in a bun and without a single wisp of impossible fluorescence.

"You know," Bell was saying as they approached, "putting a wake together's like passing a kidney stone: You think it's going to be easy, and then it just starts hurting. Remind me not to let my friends die again."

Tim's grip on Bell's arm tightened protectively, and she laughed—a dry, hurt thing.

"Don't worry. It's just how I cope—you don't laugh at the situation, you cry about it later. And I spent half an hour making this eyeliner look like a normal person's."

They passed her without a glance, and Ebenezer followed them. The specter drifted in her wake at the limits of her sight.

As the rain continued, Bell stopped and unfolded a black umbrella covered with large pink dots.

"The one time this month I say, 'Hey, let's walk!' it rains. Of course!" They continued underneath the umbrella's shadow. "Thanks, by the way. For coming with me."

"It wasn't an option—at least, not if I wanted to look in the mirror again. I'm here because of her."

Ebenezer started and had to flail to keep from falling down.

"Yeah, weird coincidence, huh? I just can't think why she was there. On Christmas Eve, too. Other than work, she doesn't…didn't go out too much." Bell snapped her fingers. "Oh! Right! Her and Marley went there all the time. She was probably just thinking. You know, wistful."

Even with her face in profile, Ebenezer could see the tears pearling on Bell's false eyelashes.

"Fuck. Oh, Christ."

"I know. I've thought about that, too."

"Was she was out there at the same time thinking? Looking? I don't know." Bell rubbed her eyes again and chuckled hollowly. "Well, God damn it. There goes my makeup."

They walked in silence for a while.

"When I was in the psych place, Ann's therapist told her some things," Tim said at last. "How it wasn't her fault, and she couldn't have known. And how bad it is to second-guess."

"I get it. But it's me we're talking about, here. I'm not so good at the letting go and letting God thing."

Tim stepped in front of her.

"No. It's bad for everyone."

Bell bowed her head.

"You know what it's like having a therapist for a mother? A *Jewish* therapist mother? Every night was new age woo-woo feelings central at my house. Every dinner was like therapy—or how her one bipolar client was, or that one guy in the hospital on—on watch. I knew what to do for suicidal friends all through high school—don't leave them alone, watch out if they suddenly get better."

"Bell."

"I mean, I get it. With Ann and you, it was okay. She didn't know. I did. If I'd just called more, or…I

185

don't know. I just don't know. If I'd dragged her to the hospital. Made her…"

Her mouth moved wordlessly. Tim pulled her into a hug.

"I just don't understand," she sobbed. "You were right there, ready to jump. Hallucinating, even. And she pulled you back. Why couldn't she pull herself back? Why couldn't someone?"

Ebenezer had felt this particular coldness in her limbs only once before—in a hospital waiting room as a Salt Lake City winter scraped through the nearly leafless trees outside. She had not expected her mother to live then. Certainly, she had not expected to be out-lived by her…and for the same reason—the same weakness, as far as she was concerned.

The rain poured down on the three of them.

"We're getting soaked," Bell noted eventually. "I don't wanna look more like hell than I have to. How about you?"

"Oh, no. You haven't seen hell until six months in the psych ward," Tim insisted. "When your beard starts eating more crumbs and soup than you do because you can't have razors, then talk to me about hell."

He smiled at her. It wasn't all that funny, but Bell still laughed with some substance before throwing her arms around him once again.

"God," she breathed. "You and Ann actually make me thankful for machine failures, you know that? If you didn't have that extra MetroCard, or if I'd walked home instead that night, you wouldn't be here now. Sharing this."

"And you wouldn't know that Ebenezer's the reason I'm here now, sharing this."

"Yeah. I just…wish she could have been here, too, you know?"

They walked on for two blocks, chatting uselessly about the weather, costume projects, distractions from the loss they carried. Ebenezer followed in silence, not caring that she was heading for her own funeral until the pair stopped in front of a sad gray building scarred by acid rain and a few haphazard tags. The tacky sign that served as its marquee read: closed for private service. Ebenezer rubbed her eyes, thinking she was mistaken.

Why were they at the Haverly Theatre?

As Bell took the first step to the old church door's, Tim stopped her.

"Are you going to be okay?"

"Hey, Tim, it's me. The hostess thing is my can of cope." Bell's grin had returned, although only a shadow of itself. "You wait for Ann while I go boss my minions, or rearrange the fruit plates or the deck chairs or something."

Tim nodded. "You know where to find me if the deck chairs get too heavy."

The theatre's foyer had the same carpet stains Ebenezer recalled—and the same faded production photos, and the same wan light filtering through the same high windows as it had five years ago. It even had the same people—at least, it had Hector and Melora waiting outside the office, looking much the same, if older.

"Hadar Rishkin?" Melora asked, offering her hand.

"That's right, but call me Bell." The seamstress shook her hand and then Hector's. "Hadar's just for taxes, banking, and my grandmother. The theatre's through there?" She pointed across the lobby.

187

"That's right. The door sticks, though. Let me show you." Hector gently steered her to it. "We just left the food on the tables when it came. You can move it if it's not right."

"The food!" Bell pressed a hand against his shoulder. "Fuck. Fuck. Fuck! I told them to deliver it at five, didn't I? Not six. I thought I said six!"

Hector's face was always exactly like a teddy bear's, down to the soft brown color and the eternally unoffended expression.

"It's no problem."

"I am so sorry," Bell insisted. "I would have been here early, too, but I couldn't find my coat, or my speech and…" A tear slid down her face bearing half that eye's mascara. "Shit. Typical neurotic Jewish girl, huh? I'm not even this stupid and guilty and apologetic usually, I—"

That teddy bear hand patted hers.

"It's okay. Really. It was just a little unloading. What are managing directors for? It's okay you're screwed up, too. We all were when we heard."

"Yeah." Bell sniffled, smearing the oil streak indelicately across her shirt.

"We're doing my new play this season, and we wanted her to audition." He sighed. "It was weird, you know? Melora just got this bad feeling when she didn't call us back or even email after a week. Bad enough she had nightmares. Ebenezer wasn't like that—she checked her voicemail every break, last time she was here. Now we know."

He tugged the door open and led Bell into the black box beyond, which smelled of mildew, mothballs, and adrenaline. The fluorescents buzzed above two battered tables on which sat unremarkable cold cuts, sweaty cheeses, and out-of-season fruit.

Bell moaned at the sight of it.

"The shit you get when you don't do it yourself. Not that anyone who's coming felt like cooking, even me."

"Well, the fruit looks fresh. At least?"

"Yeah, great. It's just gonna have to do, though. I hope she wouldn't kick my ass for this." Bell rubbed her shoulder, wincing as if trying to work out a knot. "Ah… anyway, Ebenezer's ex should be bringing her latest headshot. Is there some stand we can put it on? Like an easel?"

"Nanami, our stage manager, would know. I'll go find her. If you need anything she can't do, we'll be in the office."

As Hector took his leave, Ebenezer sat down in a corner. She started when something cold nestled down beside her—she had forgotten the genius' existence.

"Damn it, don't do that!"

The apparition seemed to take no notice, although Ebenezer couldn't tell for sure. To distract herself from the horror it instilled, she turned her attention to Bell and the tall woman emerging from behind one ratty black curtain, an easel clutched in one hand.

Belatedly, Ebenezer remembered her as a fellow classmate and one of Marley's directors, and by far the meanest. When she had become a stage manager, the actress could not guess.

"Hi," said Nanami. "Hector said you needed this?" She looked neither mean nor nice.

189

Ebenezer looked on with mounting interest as Bell chatted up the newcomer while they positioned the easel and set up several folding chairs along the theatre's eastern wall. Despite the vestiges of mascara greasing both cheeks, she was in full Bell-mode, leaping from the weather to the economy and to any number of other banalities just as she leapt through crowds of partiers. Nanami was laughing by the time Tim entered with a short Hispanic woman whom Ebenezer presumed was Ann.

As the four lined up the chairs, their conversation slowly turned to Ebenezer.

"I remember when she worked here, back when I was still directing. It was *We are Not These Hands*, I think." Nanami smoothed a black strand of hair behind an ear. "We went to school together, you know."

"Wow." Bell raised an eyebrow. "She never told me."

Nanami nodded. "Honestly, that doesn't surprise me. She was always kind of quiet like that—very aloof, even secretive, sometimes. I don't think she liked me much, or most of us."

"Yeah, people think—thought that a lot. But that was just the way she did life," Bell said. "She probably liked you fine."

"No, you were a bitch," Ebenezer insisted, but she put no heart into it. The presence at her side merely stared forward—as if it had any eyes or any interest whatsoever in human affairs.

Bell repositioned the punch bowl on its doily.

"She was a little hard to get to know sometimes, but when she got going…I have these parties. Around all the fun secular holidays, the not so fun ones like

190

Arbor Day, the religious ones like Easter and High Holy Days, because I'm a dirty agnostic—any time I can, pretty much. So, Marley used to bring her, and you're right. She was a bit aloof. At first. You gave her some time, she got into it.

"There was this one party—my Mardi Gras party, I think—where she didn't want to come at first, and by three a.m. she was the one that didn't want to leave. And this other party I did, around New Year's about a year ago, I had an open mic. We had a lot of takers, the usual stuff." She rattled them off on her fingers. "A couple jugglers, some musicians, more bad poetry than should be legal—I love my friends, but good God, none of them are poets. Even bad ones.

"And Ebenezer steps up after the last shitty round of darkity dark Gothness. 'I thought I'd do some improv,' she says. Then goes, 'Give me a noun. A scene. A concept.'

"The whole room just stares at her. And she stares back until they start shouting shit out—like 'Blue Meanies,' 'carburetors,' 'nipple hair!' And she rolled with all of them.

"You know how improv can make people homicidal when it gets boring and just keeps going on? She was up there for two hours, and no one booed her off. In fact, I had to break it up when she started to lose her voice."

She pursed her lips thoughtfully.

"You know, I think that was the best party I've ever attended." Her face abruptly reddened. "And now, fuck. She'll never do that again, and I'll never see her. Wow. Third breakdown in half an hour! Yay!"

But in a few breaths, she had calmed herself, just as more people trickled into the room. That trickle did not dry up for twenty minutes.

Ebenezer recognized a few of them from the party she had invisibly attended, most prominently Nikolai and Clea, now clad in respectable gray and green, and Mariam in a sleigh-less scooter.

"They're here just to be nice," Ebenezer informed the genius at her side.

The door opened next on a passel of people, some of whose names Ebenezer knew and others she had forgotten. Regardless, she recognized them all as actors, directors, designers and crew people from the years when she still acted.

"They're just here because Bell knows everyone," she insisted.

The Genius of the Future just sat there.

The door bumped again and let in Fred, Carl, and the woman with tight braids from her former job whom Ebenezer knew only as Right. They held the door for Lydia, who leaned heavily upon her cane with each step, then two aging women—her mother looking just five minutes shocked out of severe depression and her red-eyed grandmother looking frailer than her granddaughter remembered.

"They just came because I'm family," Ebenezer said, and regretted the words immediately. "Is there any way for them to hear me?"

Silence confirmed that there was not. Still, Ebenezer found herself running to her family's side.

"You're Ebenezer's mom?" Bell offered one large be-ringed hand. "I'm Hadar. Bell."

"She called us last week," Ebenezer's grandmother prompted when her daughter merely blinked and stared politely.

"Oh," Ebenezer's mother said at last. "That's right." Her hand came up, then dangled in mid-air like a disconnected thought.

Bell shook it nonetheless.

"It's a pleasure to meet you. Ebenezer was a good friend of mine."

"I'm glad," her mother said vacantly. "She always sounded so lonely when she called us. Forgive me, Bell. I'm not really doing well right now."

"Hey, that's fine," Bell soothed. "I was just telling Nanami and Tim—my friends—that I'm now New York's Old Faithful—I gush every ten minutes. You can pretty much set your watch by me. See?" She pointed at her eyes. "Half an hour ago, these actually had liner."

Her mother smiled thinly, but it was a pyrrhic victory for Ebenezer. Her family looked like they had not quite pulled through a hurricane.

"Mom..." Ebenezer managed.

Hiding her bandaged wrists beneath sleeves in July, her mother had always said that she hoped Ebenezer would be strong and successful—anyone but her.

"I'm sorry," she would say, whether laid out in a hospital bed or in her own. "I'm just so sorry."

Ebenezer did not need the Genius of the Past to recall her mother's eyes encircled with fatigue, and her lead-heavy voice.

"Oh, Mom," she said again—anything else felt hypocritical and insufficient.

The door bumped again, letting in a blond woman Ebenezer didn't recognize. The stranger glanced around the room, looking anxious and out of place until Ebenezer's grandmother waved her over.

"Oh, my God," the woman cried when in hearing distance. "You won't believe how stupid—I got off two streets late! Oh, sorry. I'm not interrupting, right? Or too late?"

Ebenezer just stared at the newcomer as Bell smiled. Something in the thrust of her jaw, the cast of her gray eyes—something should have been familiar.

"Not at all! We're weren't going to start until seven." Bell said. Then, her fingers snapped as she pursed her lips. "Now I sound stupid. I have the guest list here, and I don't—"

"It's okay. It was kind of last-minute." The woman took Bell's hand, looking apologetic. "I'm Ronelle. I'm Ebenezer's stepsister."

"You are fucking kidding," Ebenezer told the genius, who stared ahead as always.

Bell's smile remained polite, even as her head tilted in confusion.

"Really? Huh. I don't remember Ebenezer ever..."

"She wouldn't of," Ronelle looked down at her hands. "Basically? Our dad's a jerk. My mom's a jerk. And I'm the biggest jerk. And we probably helped make all this possible. When Dad called me up to tell me she was...I mean, I just didn't know how, you know? Sorry covers some things, but..." She shrugged and wiped at her eyes. "I couldn't ever figure out what would."

Bell rubbed her chin in contemplation.

"The thing about Ebenezer," she said at last, "is that's exactly what she'd want to hear. That you were a jerk,

194

and you screwed up her life, and you don't know what to say. No, really, it would have been like Christmas for her. Trust me." She closed Ronelle's gaping mouth with a finger and a wink. "If she was here now, you'd be her favorite person."

Basically, that was true, Ebenezer admitted. Still, Ronelle was possibly the worst person who could have shown up at her funeral.

Then came one worse.

As if on cue, Bell's head turned as the theatre's door swished open once again. Nodding to the entrants, she then turned back to Ebenezer's family.

"I'll be right back, okay?"

Although she was shaking, Ebenezer followed Bell across the room and did not turn away when the seamstress hugged Yuri and kissed Marley on both cheeks before tightly embracing her.

"I am so glad to see you both," she whispered into Marley's unbound hair.

When they separated at last, Marley's cheeks were streaked with tears; her whole face, Ebenezer realized, was scarred with salt.

"Yuri got the headshot framed." Her voice sounded dead—as dead, thought Ebenezer, as she felt now.

"I thought silver looked best, with the leaf pattern," he said weakly, holding up the picture for Bell's inspection.

Marley's expression sickened and wavered dangerously.

"Jesus. Of all the stupid things to talk about—" She exited in a clatter of heels and a cry, "I can't do this!" causing nearly everyone to look.

Yuri's lips pulled into a line as he handed Bell the picture.

"I'll go."

Bell looked after him until the door closed, then placed the picture on the easel as delicately as if it might break.

It was all too overwhelming. Ebenezer sank onto a folding chair and cradled her face in her hands.

"She shouldn't have come. I'm not her responsibility anymore." She could feel the genius hovering at her shoulder, could hear the breathing of the strange hourglass it held. "I don't want to be here. I don't want to see them, and it hurts." She looked up into the specter's face—or whatever passed for it. "I clearly failed at everything, okay? They don't need to pretend otherwise."

That wasn't it, though, and Ebenezer knew it. She sat in silence for a very long time as her family, colleagues, and friends spoke of her, sometimes in hushed and melancholy tones, sometimes breaking out in laughter around a strawberry or a plastic cup of merlot. It felt rather like watching a play, only Ebenezer could not remember when any play had made her feel so sad, humiliated, and upset at once.

"I want to go," she insisted.

A few pinches of sand tumbled down into the hourglass's gut; otherwise, the specter remained still as the grave. Ebenezer twitched uncomfortably, her own gut filled with a tumbling feeling.

Marley re-entered, clinging to Yuri's arm and looking paler than paper. Bell was at her side so quickly Ebenezer would have sworn she had teleported there.

"Oh, sweetie," she said, smoothing back Marley's bangs. "I am so, so sorry, I can't even—"

Marley held up one hand, refusing the rest of the condolence.

"I'm fine. But I really want to start now. I can't do this for very long."

"Okay," Bell patted her shoulder. "Okay." And striding to the stand, she raised her voice. "If I could just get your attention for a minute?"

Silence fell upon the room like a curtain, much to Ebenezer's gratitude. That accomplished, Bell raised her left hand in a wave with more trepidation than Ebenezer recalled ever seeing her display.

"Hi. Thanks for coming, everyone. I don't want to derail this whole thing too much with a big speech, because I wanna give one about as much as you wanna hear it. But if some of you do, well, it's open mike without the mike, basically.

"See, no matter what they say about the theatre being one small, slightly dysfunctional family, not all of us know each other, even when we all know—knew, that is, Ebenezer. So, it's a fact that we all have some story no one else knows, and my opinion that, if we let everybody know, we'll all be—a little bit less like people on a bunch of separate journeys."

She cleared her throat twice.

"So. I met Ebenezer doing a reading of *Antistrophe*. Basically, it was your typical retelling of *Antigone*, set in high school. With lesbians. And a principal on loan from the Westboro Baptist Church. And guns. And talking vaginas. And more *fuck you's* than any of us could count. If you missed it, congratulations."

197

There was a smattering of chuckles, and Bell gave a grin.

"Somebody thought this was a great idea because a sixteen-year-old boy wrote it, and thought Ebenezer and I should play the leads because we needed money. And the sixteen-year-old, who shall remain nameless, thought he was Arthur Miller because he got a director and a free hotel stay.

"It went about as well as you'd expect. The kid showed up stoned for one rehearsal and stormed out during another when I told him a line didn't make sense. The director called five minutes to go talk the *enfant terrible* down.

"I looked at Ebenezer and said—I don't remember what, exactly, but that the whole thing just sucked and we should quit, and fuck the money. And, really calm, she says, 'I respect my job too much for that. I respect myself too much.'

"The kid got sent home before the festival was over for walking out during a better reading of a better play. We got our paychecks, and that was that."

Bell sniffed a few times until her composure returned.

"And that was Ebenezer. She cared about things, and she wanted. She wanted so *much*." Her voice cracked into a cough. "She was an artist. She was my friend. I loved her like myself. Anyway. That's all." Stepping aside, she gestured to the space. "Your turn."

Marley was crying into Yuri's chest, and she was not the only one. But eventually, Lydia stepped forward to relate a story about a day in class, this one involving a power outage during a scene. Another fol-

lowed, and another: her mother speaking of her Christmas recitations; Fred speaking of her hard work. One
after another, the memories flooded up around her
until she knew that she would drown.

Throughout, Marley huddled in her boyfriend's
arms and wept.

"Please," Ebenezer whispered. "I can't stay here. I
can't listen to them lie like this after doing this to them.
I'm not who they think I was."

The genius seemed to turn its head.

"Bell didn't understand. None of them do. Neither did I. I didn't respect my work. I didn't respect
myself. I respected…" The word clawed through her
mind at last. "Respect. I respected respect."

The specter stared at her wordlessly.

"Oh, God," Ebenezer looked back at the room.
Marley was speaking at the front now, but the words
were distorted, as if spoken under water. Something
cold and terrifying slid onto Ebenezer's shoulders, and
she turned to find the spirit pressed against her. A keyhole was manifesting in the void of its chest.

Ebenezer flinched.

"Oh, God. It's all my fault. I can't—stop staring at
me! Don't you get it? If you know the future, you know
what I've been through. And you know what it's pushed
me—what *I've* pushed me to! It's all just broken. I can't
fix this! So why are we here? Why can't you just bury
me and let me—"

The keyhole had enlarged far enough Ebenezer
could see through it—low clouds and, through the
gloom, something long, white, and too familiar. She
tried to pull away, but the genius pulled back, and her

199

embrace was like a riptide. As Ebenezer fell through into that landscape Marley's voice broke through the fog at last.

"There was just nothing anyone could do to save her. Nothing was enough."

Scene V

Enough

There was no nausea, just coldness; its progress was like an ice floe through her arteries, crystallizing blood, tissue, and marrow. Ebenezer shivered and hugged herself; in moments, her shivering gave way to a torpor, then a leadenness.

"Where are we now?" she asked the genius at her side before realizing she needn't have bothered.

The mist parted as if by command to reveal a tombstone—white as a bleached skull and new, its colorlessness emanating from inside its cold granite.

Ebenezer did not need to look at the genius to know to whom the grave belonged. Yet when she did, its left arm was outstretched like a signpost. In the right hand, held close to its body, the hourglass's breathing had speeded up. So, too, the fall of sand. Expressionlessly, Ebenezer watched the white granules dune at the bottom.

The heaviness spread into her wrists and ankles, and Ebenezer knew she was dying.

"That's mine."

The genius inclined its head, although Ebenezer had not asked a question. Cautiously, as if the cold slab might vanish with one wrong move, she walked toward it, each step weighing more than the previous one.

Many years ago, while waiting in yet one more nondescript hospital room, Ebenezer had swung her legs and wondered what death would feel like—if it would hurt very much or feel like sinking into blankets after four hours of homework; if it felt different to die alone or among friends; if it hurt less when one made it happen or more.

As she neared her own grave, however, she concluded that it felt heavier than any of these, especially in her joints and in her wrists. Dimly, she wondered if the past resided in these places, corroding every movement until the body crumbled like a rusting bridge. It would certainly explain why she was tired from the inside out, so unlike just fourteen years ago.

And she was so very tired. The tombstone looked so smooth and comforting, a thing all of light, and no pain. She was so very tired of that, too.

Vaguely, Ebenezer wondered how to die in this genius's shadow world. She saw no bridge, no river spreading black and deep and painless.

Just stand upon it.

She did not stop to wonder whether the thought came from her or from the spirit at her back. With every bit of her remaining will, Ebenezer stepped onto the stone and bowed her head. It seemed the proper thing to do.

"I'm ready," she told the genius, for she now knew its true identity.

The fog stilled on her neck and cheeks, and the air itself hesitated. Then, something heavy and cold spilled from her hands as if it had been waiting there for years. As it clanked at her feet, Ebenezer glanced down.

Two chains now bound her to the stone. Each was a good inch thick and long enough to coil upon itself like the chill body of a python. Her heart kicked hard against her ribs for a few seconds before despair settled down on her once again. There was no point in terror at this point, even of the unfamiliar and unsettling. She repeated these words to herself as she bowed her head again and waited for whatever would come for her.

It did not come as she expected, but the end was fitting, nonetheless. The manacles pulled taut about her wrists, and her feet began to sink into the soft, star-bright stone. It wasn't like the blankets of her youth, or even like startling from sleep. It felt cold, enormous as a cathedral's yawn. It made her want to start extinguishing herself and all the memories that stung her.

The white-tiled hospitals and their ammonia stench went first, followed closely by the schoolyard taunts and punches and all their adrenaline and tears. Ebenezer had no regrets for these, or for the close and sweaty high school halls that followed. Four years of fretting on the university's stages were just as easy to lay by—the parts had been minimal, the professors stiff-lipped and stuffed with disappointment, the connections she had made uneasy and unhelpful post-graduation.

Everything that came after was just as hurtful, just as forgettable.

The people—Ebenezer banished them even faster than she thought she could have. But it was an easy thing, she reflected, when she had ruined all of their lives. Even memories of Marley and Bell were easy to push off; one had moved beyond her, one had never needed her at all. Everything after was no different—the dusty stages and late nights, the slim salaries and dead-pan reviews, the eventual sag into an office chair. How was any of that different from this slide into the earth?

In fact, had it not started even sooner, Ebenezer asked herself. When she had picked Introduction to Drama instead of Introduction to Computers? In her absurd, teenage living room declarations? Or in the words that she declaimed?

Her mind now felt as black and cold as the Hud-son River, but one figure remained among the ice floes. In the middle of the pulsing water stood her fourteen-year-old self, straight as a candle, strangely just as bright. She carried a battered copy of *Romeo and Ju-liet* and was in the midst of another humiliating reci-tation.

O, then, I see Queen Mab hath been with you.
She is the fairies' midwife, and she comes
In shape no bigger than an agate-stone
On the fore-finger of an alderman,
Drawn with a team of little atomies
Athwart men's noses as they lie asleep...

"Go away," Ebenezer told her.

The girl glanced up from her reading, almost cu-riously, but her overacting did not cease.

Her wagon-spokes made of long spinners' legs,
The cover of the wings of grasshoppers,
The traces of the smallest spider's web,

The collars of the moonshine's watery beams,
Her whip of cricket's bone; the lash of film;
Her waggoner a small grey-coated gnat,
Not half so big as a round little worm
Prick'd from the lazy finger of a maid...

Her older self repeated the exhortation, to no effect.

"Why won't you leave?" she whispered.

Hearing her anguish perhaps, the memory marked the page with an index finger.

"Shh," she admonished, although gently. "I'm getting to the best part. Tryouts are tomorrow," she explained when her future incarnation merely stared at her. "I don't want to mess this up."

"It doesn't matter —"

"Shhhhhh!"

"None of this matters!" Ebenezer slapped the book away. "Don't you understand that now?"

The teenager sighed petulantly as she stooped and retrieved the play from the ebbing river water, its pages miraculously undamaged.

"Of course it matters," she insisted. "It's only the most important thing in the world!"

Ebenezer readied herself to scold again, but her younger self held up a hand.

"It's the most important thing," she said again, with such a look of grown-up intensity that Ebenezer wondered at it. Without another word, her younger self turned and walked into the rushing darkness, which lightened markedly with each step.

Ebenezer had not thought of the classroom for well over a decade, but it loomed before her now, fully formed as had been each of her memories on this strange night. The room's split-pea carpet and powdery chalkboard had obviously changed little from their installation at least two decades ago.

For all Ebenezer knew, it was that way even now.

Plump cotton balls of snowflakes drifted past the window as the ninth graders removed thick readers from their satchels and backpacks, the covers just as frayed and sickly green as the unhappy, glue-spotted thing beneath their boots and sneakers.

It was December. Ebenezer knew that much because a holiday humor hung over the place as surely as the clouds lowered outside—and, for that matter, because a Santa hat topped Ms. Angelos' perpetually disheveled, mouse-brown perm, in spite of school regulations. In addition, red-and-green-iced cupcakes perched on each desk like festive igloos, which a few greedy hands had already disheveled.

Her younger self had taken a front seat and opened the hideous book well before the teacher had asked, telegraphing her social isolation and gaucheness so effectively Ebenezer cringed.

The English teacher crossed the T on "Juliet" with a flourish before turning her back to the ancient chalkboard.

"Quiet, please," she called, and when the chatter did not ebb: "Quiet! Class, I know that break's in two days, and we're all excited, especially me. But we really have to finish this act before the party tomorrow."

"Why?" called out one surly boy, whose name Ebenezer did not recall. But there was always one in every class.

"It's in my contract." Ms. Angelos shrugged. "And because I like to annoy you, Levi, of course."

The class chuckled, and the boy grinned.

"Okay, we left off on page six-oh-eight. Ebenezer, you'll be Benvolio again? Juan, you'll be Romeo, and Levi—"

"Mercutio. Gotcha!" Levi aimed a finger-gun for his teacher and clicked his tongue.

The teacher rolled her eyes.

"Uintah, will you do stage directions?" When the girl nodded, Ms. Angelos leaned back against her desk and fondly watched them read.

"This is ridiculous."

Her younger self turned in her seat and shushed her once again.

"We both know how this ends." Ebenezer sighed. "You're going to ham up your lines and mispronounce *prolixity* and *betake* and feel stupid all day."

"Sometimes you don't remember how things went," the teen insisted. "'The date is out of such prolexity—'"

"Pro*lix*ity," Ms. Angelos kindly corrected.

"The date is out of such prolixity/We'll have no Cupid hoodwink'd with a scarf," the teenager read again, red scattering across her cheeks. Her words were no less stilted for her enthusiasm.

Ebenezer rolled her eyes and mouthed *I told you*, but her young self read on, patently ignoring her.

As the reading continued, Ebenezer stroked her hand across the back of her past self's chair and wondered why she was here. Dying was rumored to make a life clip past like a film reel, not focus like a camera lens, hard upon one memory.

207

"In case you hadn't noticed, I'm right in the middle of—"

"Don't go yet," her young self interrupted without turning around. Then importuning, "Please."

Sighing, Ebenezer remained as teen after teen rattled out his or her lines. It was a stupid way to spend one's last breathing minutes, she thought; even Levi, with all his smarmy charm, was bad.

"This is pointless," she tried again, but her young self was not listening. She was sitting straight-backed in her chair and leaning so intently over her book that Ebenezer wondered if it had just done a trick.

"Drawn with a team of little atomies/Athwart men's noses as they lie asleep," Levi intoned.

Something stirred in Ebenezer's chest, like the soft paws of a mouse. She found herself leaning over her younger self's shoulders, reading each word as the boy droned it.

Her wagon-spokes made of long spiders' legs,
The cover of the wings of grasshoppers,
The traces of the smallest spider's web,
The collars of the moonshine's watery beams,
Her whip of cricket's bone, the lash of film,
Her wagoner a small grey-coated gnat,
Not so big as a round little worm
Prick'd from the lazy finger of a maid…

The mouse paws scampered, became a herd, became a drubbing in her stomach, then her chest and bones.

And in this state she gallops night by night

208

Through lovers' brains, and then they dream
    of love;
O'er courtiers' knees, that dream on court'sies
    straight,
O'er lawyers' fingers, who straight dream on fees,
O'er ladies ' lips, who straight on kisses dream,
Which oft the angry Mab with blisters plagues,
Because their breaths with sweetmeats tainted
    are.

The air felt charged. Ebenezer gulped and could not look away from the torn and inky page beneath her. The words tumbled past; her eyes had no choice but to follow, her mouth no choice but to form around each consonant and plosive, over each wide O.

They're just words. They just cause trouble, she told herself, knowing full well this was a lie.

As her younger self murmured the words beneath her breath, Ebenezer felt them engulf her like fleece blankets—softer and far warmer than she had imagined death. Although Levi spoke in the stop-and-go of youth, she heard the iambs pulse, steady as a slow, great heart.

"Do you hear it?" young Ebenezer whispered.

Her present self nodded.

"It's beautiful," the teen sighed with the hope and joy of unbound youth, and Ebenezer shivered. "It's old, but beautiful. Like those Depression bottles in Aunt Vona's windows. It's like…I don't know…like I'm reaching out my hand and touching something… something…" She chewed her lip, frustrated.

"Something bigger," Ebenezer finished for her.

Something like a waterfall broke free then. In the crashing down, she understood.

"It isn't that it's old, or even beautiful. It's like music. Like the songs Aunt Vona sang that Great-grandma sung to her, and her grandmother, and her grandmother. Maybe all the way back to the pioneer days—probably long before, maybe even when Shakespeare was writing this.

"People spoke this four hundred years ago, and people still shiver at it now. These stories, speaking them—it's the only way we know each other. It's the only way we know anybody, the only way we touch." Her cheeks were moist, and the classroom wavered. "That's why," she whispered as the water tumbled over her.

The recitation had ended some time ago without her notice. From her seat, the young girl smiled mischievously.

"Peace, peace, Mercutio, peace!" she said. "Thou talk'st of nothing."

"No," Ebenezer insisted. "Not nothing. It means everything."

The girl's smile brightened even as she faded, taking the classroom with her.

"No, don't go." Ebenezer reached for her hand but could not touch it. "There's so much more."

"You'll be fine," her vanishing self reassured her.

"It's the reason I did everything, yes, but I don't know how! I don't know how to make it enough. I don't know how to do it anymore!" Ebenezer cried. As the girl disappeared completely, she stretched her arm as far as it would go.

Instead of mist and water, cold stone met her fingertips. Gasping, Ebenezer opened her eyes. She found herself encased mid-thigh in the stone, her hands mere inches from its rim. And she was still sinking.

"I don't know how," she pleaded with the open air. "I don't know what to do!"

The slab jolted again, and Ebenezer slid down with it. The chains dug into her wrists as her palms slammed against the granite and her fingers spread like the legs of a wounded spider. The force of the motion threw her torso forward; only a spine-popping jerk spared her head from the tombstone.

Until she pulled back, Ebenezer had not read its looming inscription, thinking it nothing but the obvious. The jolt, however, made her face not her name carved in those stencil lines, but a solution that hit like a thunder stone.

ACT

And with that one word, she made her decision. "Enough," she said. "Enough."

Her hands pressed against the granite. Ebenezer pushed and pushed, muscles screaming, joints screaming, mouth screaming against the weight that closed her in. She thrashed and jerked with every tendon, every sinew.

As she fought against the grave, the heaviness she had dragged for years seemed to drop away. The chains strained against her skin until bones crunched, and then the manacles snapped with a cold and brittle sound. Moving freer now, Ebenezer dug her fingers into the stone as nails split and palms gaped in hot surprise.

"Enough!" The word tore from her all the while like a battle cry. "Enough!"

Her feet struggled in their prison until it cracked like a fault line. Yelling, and with shoulders aching nearly to dislocation, Ebenezer tore free of the grave and pitched to her left. Her shoulder blade landed on soft, dewy grass, and her legs swung clear of the trap. Rolling to a crouch, she saw the granite liquefy and close over the gap she had left, becoming solid once again.

Trembling, Ebenezer stumbled to her feet. As she steadied herself, a cold hand rested on her shoulder. The genius stood behind her, impossibly tall even with its head tilted. Ebenezer thought she saw a grin in the darkness of the cowl.

"No," she told it. When the hands squeezed tighter, she snapped, "I am not going back in there!" before slamming her bleeding palms into its chest.

The hands remained, even after Ebenezer's shoves turned into blows. At last, sore and exhausted from her climb, she fell against the billowing scrim of the figure's robes, huffing painful breaths.

"I'm scared," she gasped as her eyes stung again. "I'm just so scared."

She did not flinch as one spectral? hand slipped into the curve of her aching back, or even when the other carded her tangled hair. Stepping further into the genius's embrace, Ebenezer tucked her head onto its breast.

"God, everything's so fucked up right now. How am I ever going to fix it?"

212

The question had been rhetorical, and even if it had not been, Ebenezer had not expected the genius to tilt its head to look into her face.

"Go forward," the Genius of the Future whispered, and Ebenezer found herself caught up in a kiss. Her lips pressed back in surprise, then parted as her arms slowly wrapped around the figure's waist.

Like a canyon wind, the kiss left her gasping. Or so she thought, until she felt the air pull back her cheeks. The ghostly images swimming in the genius's body were flickering like a fireplace. As Ebenezer stared, Marley and Yuri drifted past, then Fred and her co-workers, the Cratchits at their TV trays with Martha dozing in her chair; a bare stage lit by a floodlight; a crowded room and finally, Bell, looking up from a sewing machine, her round face bare of makeup, her expression one of surprise, confusion, then delight.

"Ebenezer!" she exclaimed before the image tore into snow-brightness and Ebenezer felt herself falling through the genius's robes.

It felt a bit like stumbling into and then through a curtain as she sped through the darkness. The brightness ahead was coming into focus. As Ebenezer fell, the picture became sharp, became clear.

Became her sun-flooded apartment.

ACT V

The Past, Present, and Future

Scene I

I Don't Know What to Do

The morning light poured through the windows like clear broth as Ebenezer rubbed her eyes, her face, her arms and on. Her blood still flowed, and while her hands bore no traces of grave-struggle, the blankets were twisted through her legs and arms like chains.

Shuddering, Ebenezer kicked them all away and found yesterday's black skirt and socks and her winter coat beneath. Odd, she thought. Had she really gone to bed without throwing it over a chair back?

Regardless, that explained the sweat running down her like baptism.

She stood slowly, as if anticipating a migraine, surprised the strange dreams' afterimages had not caused one. Or was she still dreaming? The thought compelled her to the window in little cat-like steps.

The ghost town of last night, a red Utah sand storm, even a fall of gasping trout would not have surprised her more than the overcast New York morning she discovered. It had snowed last night, and heavily, but the ploughs had done their work; and the cavalcade of taxis, cars, and buses honked along as usual, although perhaps with a little of the silence only a winter holiday can bring. The salted sidewalks crunched with fewer people, too.

Ebenezer stared through the glass and shook her head again and again. It was Christmas morning. She was alive.

"But what *that*?" she asked several times aloud. "What the hell was that?"

The streets stared back at her. A shower, she decided. A shower would clear her head, at least. Sure enough, the hot water eased the stiffness in her neck (from sleeplessness or night walking?) and left her feeling alert and fresh, if still confused.

She tried tea next, peppermint and too steamy to drink at first. By the time the kettle shrilled, the snow had returned in those big cotton puffs that always put her in a contemplative mood. Ebenezer pulled a chair to the window and watched them attentively as the cup cooled on the sill.

"Go forward," she repeated. As if doing that was easy. But then, maybe that was the point.

She stared into the snow and sipped her tea. She stared past the dregs of two mugs and well into a third, her thoughts drifting through the whiteness, through memory, through a dozen different possibilities, all of which seemed real and far away…but exciting.

She had forgotten the pin-pricks of excitement.

Somehow, through her reverie, Ebenezer heard the jarring of the telephone. Thankful for the interruption, she caught the receiver up on the third ring without even glancing at the name.

"Hi, you've reached Marley and Ebenezer," Marley's voice chirped from the machine. "We can't come to the pho—"

Wincing, Ebenezer cut the ghost off with a frantic push of a button.

"Hi! Hello. Sorry about that."

"Hi, honey. Merry Christmas."

"Mom?" Smoothing a snarly lock from her eyes, Ebenezer eased herself back into the chair. She was answered by a quick intake of breath.

"Oh, Ebbie, I'm sorry! It's not too early there, is it?"

"Mom, it's—"

"Because I always forget if you're ahead of me, or behind, or what. Especially with this new thing they've put me on. You're two hours ahead of Mountain Time, right?"

"Yes, Mom. It's..." Ebenezer glanced at the VCR's clock. "Wow. It's already eleven."

"Oh, good," Her mother sighed, sounding relieved. "Anyway, I know you're busy, so I won't keep you long. Me and Gramma just wanted to wish you and Marley a Merry Christmas."

"Marley..." Ebenezer bit her lip.

"Yeah, can you put her on?"

"Um..."

"Is she gone now?"

"Kind of..." Ebenezer felt the heat rise in her chest again. The sob barked out before she could control it.

"Honey, what is it?" Her mother's voice pitched up in concern, then with increasing panic. "Is she okay? She's not hurt, is she?"

"No." Ebenezer hiccupped. "No, it's not like that. But I am, Mom. It just hurts so much." She didn't want it to happen, but the whole story poured out unbid-

219

den then, with such speed and force her mother asked her to slow down, to repeat and breathe. She said little else until her daughter choked out those last, final and dreadful words:

"And…it's been a week, and she has a boyfriend! Who she was already looking at when I was…when I was busy basically sulking and ignoring her, and of course she would. Oh Christ, Mom. I really fucked up."

Ebenezer's mother waited to speak until her daughter had ceased repeating this last sentence.

"Oh, Ebbie, I'm so sorry. Do you want me to fly down there?" The tenderness in her voice reminded Ebenezer of strong arms and a soft, round face that looked as though it had forgotten how to smile. Guilt rose like a tidal wave, and she wept harder.

Her mother soothed and shushed wordlessly.

"I wish you'd called me," she said at last.

Ebenezer coughed away some phlegm.

"You didn't need to hear about all this. I'm sorry you're hearing about it now."

"How come?"

Ebenezer struggled for an answer that wouldn't be uncomfortable.

"Because I'm an adult. I can take care of this. I should be able to take care of this."

Her mother's laugh was surprisingly light.

"And you don't think I'm an adult?"

"It's not…that isn't what I meant, Mom."

"Ebbie." Her voice had that serious tone now that was at once like gold and steel, the tone she typically reserved for nosy relatives, doctors, and Mormon missionaries. "Ebbie. I'm fine. Really."

"Fine like you were when you locked yourself in the bathroom with Uncle Von's rifle?" Ebenezer winced. "I'm sorry. That was…I shouldn't have…I just meant…"

"That was a very long time ago. Before Prozac and Celexa. Before I even knew what was really wrong."

Ebenezer sighed another round of tears back down.

"But neither of them worked."

She could almost hear her mother shrugging.

"That's just the med dance, honey. It doesn't mean I can't do anything else. Or that you can't call me when you don't have anything happy to say."

"But that's always."

"Well, sometimes that's life. But Gramma and I love you, all right?"

"All right," Ebenezer scrubbed the bathrobe's terrycloth sleeve against her nose, still feeling young, but less embarrassed now. She managed a throaty laugh. "Well, so my life sucks. How's yours?"

"Gramma's fine. I'm fine, though I could really do without the insomnia. We went to Sizzler Christmas Eve with Uncle Von and Aunt Fawna and their daughter. It was mostly real quiet."

But the catch in her voice, that tension like the dry air before a rainstorm, told Ebenezer otherwise. Sure enough, it came before she could prepare herself.

"I really hate to drop this on you now, especially when you're feeling so bad."

"Is it Gramma?"

"Hm? Oh, no, she's fine. It's Ronelle."

Ebenezer realized her mouth was hanging open only when her mother said, "Hello? Are you still there?"

"Uh—sorry. What about her?"

"She came out to see us on the twenty-third with her boyfriend and her kid—she's six, and just so smart. She reminds me a lot of you, actually. Like you were at that age."

"Ronelle—she's got a kid?" Ebenezer blinked and blinked, and still the truth unfolded as the genius had shown it, and not quite.

"Uh-huh. Cassandra. I guess that breaks the Utah name tradition." Her mother's voice now took on notes of quicksilver, sliding in all directions. "She asked how you were doing. She's seen some things—clippings from the college newspaper, your name in playbills. She's not like that last time, when you visited Dad. She's kicked the drugs. Joined the church. Got Cassie baptized.

"She said she was trying to do—she said amends for what she did before she sobered up. And that she owes you an apology, and a lot more. She said, if you wanted—and only if you did—she'd like to get to know you better, even be your friend. But only if you wanted."

When Ebenezer did not reply, her mother continued. "Hon, I know you don't like her. I'm not even sure what I think about all this. I just know she had this look in her eyes like I get when I'm depressed and I think I've ruined everybody's life. I know *that's* not fake, at least. Ebbie,

"I didn't even want to tell you about this. I thought I wouldn't, especially not on Christmas. But I figured, you can take care of it. You're so much stronger than you give yourself credit for."

Ebenezer's eyes were dewing again, despite her blinking.

"What's her number?"

"Really?"

"She left one, right? Or an email?"

Her mother excused herself to locate the Post-It note, then read both number and email off slowly, making sure Ebenezer made no mistakes on any number or letter.

"It's up to you two how you handle it, but I really hope it works out. It would be nice for you to finally have a sister."

Ebenezer had deduced as much.

"Mom? I don't want to change the subject like an ass, but I really need to talk about something happier now. I think we both do."

Her mother seemed only too happy to agree.

Ebenezer had nothing but her restless dreams to share, and not quite understanding them herself, she decided not to make her mother worry needlessly, at worst, or bore her at best. Rather, she let her mother talk about her art classes and her job at the new hotel, and about her own restlessness.

"Gramma and I've been talking, Ebbie. Of course, there's no chance we'll sell the house in this market. But when it recovers, we're thinking of something smaller, maybe in Salt Lake. Like an apartment. I'm just not interested in gardening anymore, and the yard's really too much for Gramma to keep up by herself.

"Vernal's just changing so much, it's practically a big city now, anyway. They say there's better jobs in Salt Lake, too. I don't want to keep you, though. You probably have a lot you want to do today."

The snow was falling softer now, in little pinpricks; just watching it made Ebenezer feel slow and contemplative, and very much in want of chocolate.

"I wasn't planning on anything much. I didn't sleep so well last night, and I don't think anyone really wants to see me right now."

"Why not?"

"I haven't been the easiest person to deal with lately. You know what that's like."

"Even more than you'd think," her mom said.

Ebenezer walked back to the window, cradling the cordless phone against her shoulder.

"It would be nice to see Marley."

"Too soon for both of you?"

"She just...she didn't leave an address or a number, and I'm probably blocked from her email and everything else online. So, I don't know when *won't* be too soon. Maybe never."

"It never helps to say things will get better, so I won't. I'll just say I'm sorry. And that we all make mistakes, and usually they're not permanent, even if they feel that way."

"I know. I know that. Everything just feels like a platitude now, though."

"Then you're really not going to like this—I believe in you. Gramma believes in you. Everybody out here does, even if they don't really understand theatre. And Ronelle believes in you, if you want her to. You'll work this out, or it just won't be something you can fix. And life will go on. Of course it's harder to think that than it sounds; I wouldn't need therapy otherwise."

For the first time that morning, Ebenezer smiled. It was a weak birth, pale and scarcely moving, whether the first in a long line of smiles or the last of its generation, she could not have said.

"Yes. It doesn't help right now. But I'll remember it."

"Remember that we love you, okay? No matter what."

"I love you, too, Mom. All of you." And for the first time in years, Ebenezer said it without awkwardness or guilty squirming.

Then there was little more to say, but to repeat the benediction to her grandmother after an abbreviated repeat of the previous discussion.

"If I were you, I'd go find Marley and give her a piece of my mind." The image of her grandmother shaking one weathered fist mothered another smile on Ebenezer's chapped lips. "Ignoring you like that just isn't right, no matter what you did."

"Well, it's not that easy," Ebenezer said as she re-filled the tea kettle. "People get hurt, and…and I don't know."

Her grandmother snorted.

"I still think you should ask around," she said before wishing her granddaughter a Merry Christmas and much love "in spite of that young woman" before hanging up.

Leaving the handset on the countertop, Ebenezer stared at the burner coil until her eyes blurred. If her night traveling had been more than a strange dream, as she was now fully convinced, Marley lived in Spanish Harlem now—on East 100th Street, if she correctly recalled the sign she had glimpsed in free fall. Regardless, she was certain she would recognize the gabled building on first sight.

"But I'm not going to," she told the empty room. "It's weird. It's creepy. I'm not a lot of good things, but I'm not a stalker, either."

225

But it would only take a minute, a part of her insisted. *And no matter what, Gramma's right—you deserve some closure.*

"And apparently, a restraining order." The kettle shrilled as if in agreement, and Ebenezer pulled it from the range and turned off the heat. "But it might be worth it, just to…say goodbye, I guess."

Overall, it was a stupid, stupid idea.

Five minutes later, she had dressed and grabbed her coat.

Scene II

Christmas Day

Despite the flurries, the afternoon was crisp, if indecisive. The alternating patches of sunlight and snow-hanging cloud fitted her situation so perfectly, Ebenezer could think of nothing better than to walk beneath them on her journey up and across Manhattan. A taxi would have been beyond her means, and the bus warmer but no less crowded and hated than usual.

So, she moved through the streets feeling both dreamy and nervous, more aware than she had ever been of the city's smells and colors, of the people crowding past laden with food and presents, Styrofoam cups filled with coffee or rattling with pennies, with stories she would never know that she nonetheless wanted to learn.

The thought delighted and surprised her, despite the anxiety coiling in her chest; she had not felt such wonderment in years, perhaps not since her teens. With each step came a new thought, some large, some small, but equally profound. The city smelled like spice and excitement here, and she hated being silent. Icicles were, indeed, beautiful, and her job was no longer worth it.

As she turned onto Marley's street, the greatest of these revelations ran into her full-tilt, with all the force of a subway train and a hand drifting onto her shoulder with the grace of a last autumn leaf. She was not going to cry when she saw her. Afterwards, most likely she would, but not now. She was not going to scream, either, or beg, or cause a scene. It would, perhaps, have been good drama, but she no longer needed it.

As she climbed the steps, Ebenezer wondered whether or not she still needed Marley. As she scanned the buzzer for Yuri Biryukov, she did not expect to find an answer.

She also did not expect Marley to find *her*.

"Ebenezer?"

But there she was, standing two feet from the stoop, a grocery bag clutched against her chest and her long red hair spilling out from her beret and down over a gray wool coat Ebenezer did not recognize. She wore her usual low-heeled boots, and a shocked expression that was rapidly shifting to annoyance.

Not knowing what else to do, Ebenezer held both of her gloved hands up in a gesture of truce.

"I'm not here to argue," she tried.

"Right. You're just here to yell, and pout, and guilt me. I get it. Thanks for the present, but I don't want it."

The bottom of grocery bag began to tear as Marley, rolling her eyes, attempted to push past her ex-girlfriend to the door. As she rifled through her purse to find her keys, however, the brown paper split like a mouth telling a secret, and produce, spice cans, and a shrink-wrapped chicken breast scattered down the concrete steps. An unfortunate box of chocolates burst on impact, scattering its contents in a rain of silver balls.

"God damn it!" Marley shot an accusatory glare at Ebenezer before tearing off her coat and folding it up like a sack.

"Let me help," her ex offered, one pomegranate already in hand.

"I don't need your help." But Marley didn't slap the fruit away as they filled the wool with food. The chocolates, strewn and smashed upon the ice like broken ornaments, were a hopeless loss.

"Do you live here now?" Even as she said it, Ebenezer realized her choice of conversation was a bad one.

"A friend of a friend's roommate just left for grad school. She needed help with rent, I needed a new apartment. Did Bell put you up to this? Because she really needs to mind her own damn business and not give out addresses that aren't supposed to be given out. Tell her that."

"She didn't," Ebenezer insisted. "Things just get around sometimes."

"Then tell whoever it was to stay out of it!" Marley snapped. "And stop being creepy and nosy. Over means over, not maybe, or I'll think about it, or maybe she'll reconsider if I grow up and stop expecting everything to be handed to me because I want it and—"

"I know."

Marley's jaw dropped.

"What?"

"I know that," Ebenezer said as gently as she could. "I screwed up. And I'm sorry."

Marley's eyes widened, and she nearly dropped her groceries again. After staring at Ebenezer for a moment, she said, "Okay. So, what's the punchline?"

Ebenezer shook her head.

"I'm being serious. I blew all the chances you gave me, and some things just…I wish it had ended differently, of course I do. But it didn't work that way, because love doesn't come back no matter how hard you wish. The fact I did more of my share to kick it out probably had a lot to do with that, too."

Marley stared at her and just said, "Oh."

Ebenezer shrugged and toed a smashed chocolate ball helplessly.

"I know you don't want to see me now, and maybe now includes ever again. I know why you don't want to, and I don't like it. I'm not happy about it."

"I understand that," Marley said quietly. "You don't have to be, Ebbie. Nobody asked you to be."

"I know. But I have to understand your reasons and respect them. That's why I came here. To say I do."

Marley nodded dumbly.

"Yeah. That's only fair. I didn't…I guess I didn't really even give you a chance to say it when I left. Or anything at all, really." She sighed and tucked the wool bundle of groceries against her hip. "Ebbie, you're not the only one who…you know?"

The obvious question hovered above her tongue, but Ebenezer gulped it down.

"If you ever want to talk."

"I know. In time, I hope I can."

Ebenezer offered her hand, and after only the briefest hesitation, Marley took it and pressed it between hers.

"Merry Christmas, Marl. Thanks for not calling the police."

A tear coursed down Marley's cheek, and then another.

"You're welcome, Ebbie. Merry Christmas. I didn't really get you anything, but…" She opened the coat and removed a mango. "I know they're your favorite. And we don't need all of them for Christmas dinner. You, um, you probably know about Yuri, too, right? From whoever told you…"

"Yes. I know." Ebenezer closed her hands around the fruit's cold skin. "Maybe I can meet him again someday. When it hurts less."

"Someday," Marley echoed, and her former girlfriend couldn't tell if it was acknowledgement or promise.

"Someday," she repeated nonetheless. "Thanks for the mango."

And that was it. She held the door as Marley struggled through with her burden, then turned away respectfully after closing it behind her. The snow had begun again, the little chilly flakes swirling down in what felt like loneliness and confusion. It seemed fitting, decided Ebenezer, for them and not Marley to hear her farewell.

"I love you. I think I always will, in a way."

She didn't care whether or not the passers-by saw her tears. By the time she reached Park Avenue they had vanished, anyway, although Ebenezer knew they would return for months, perhaps for years, and that they would not spare Marley any visits, either.

Regardless, she clutched the mango between her palms like a mending heart as she walked through the snow and sludge towards the West Side, to home.

Home. It was a strange realization, that an apartment that had once held so much could still be home now that it contained only an abundance of memories. There would be more tea and leftover hamburger, a Christmas movie on television filled with light and love and all the warm ridiculousness of the season.

Ebenezer was alone this Christmas, yes, but not lonely. No, she told herself, not lonely at all. She had too much to think about for that—too much to consider, and far too much to change in the days ahead. The first of these thoughts buzzed in her head like bees as she crossed the snow-hung island, head up against the wind, not looking back.

Ebenezer had been wrong about Marley—Marley lived. She lived in memory and possibility. *And so do I*, Ebenezer realized. *So do I.*

Snow settled in her hair like jewels.

Scene III

Let Me In

Christmas Day passed as she thought it would—so slow, heavy, and snowy that she fully expected another upheaval of dreams when she nestled into her own bed that night for the first time in a week. Instead there was a deep, black peacefulness and a giddy dream of dancing penguins abruptly cut short by a blast of "My Chemical Romance" from her desktop alarm.

After showering and skipping breakfast as usual, Ebenezer stepped into a curtain of snow and promptly turned about and down into the subway. Huddled between the jostling bodies, she inhaled cologne, sweat, deodorant, and dirt as she counted the blocks. It would never be anything less than unnerving, but today she had much more to think about than the crunch of bodies. Her job loomed like a shadow just three stops away.

She did not know what to do about it yet, except to note that she would rather not have to do anything. Finding another job in this economy seemed slightly less likely than landing another role; on the other hand, the possibility of her yelling at another customer was even more remote. Two weeks, she figured; two weeks before her numbers fell through the basement and Trent would gleefully replace her with another unhappy actor—or perhaps the balding white man, if he hadn't died from a coronary yet.

The doors beeped open, and Ebenezer swept out onto the platform with the rest of the workday crowd. Whoever said quitting a hated job would make you free had obviously never worked a single day, she decided.

The cubicle farm was clack-clack-clacking away when she entered, and its denizens' expressions hovered between perky, stiff, or sloppily hung over. As she slid into the chair by her computer, Ebenezer felt her face twitch and fail to freeze into its usual forced smile. Feeling more alien than she ever had at this job, she pulled up her call list and dialed the first of the day's numbers.

Happily, from two to five p.m., most of them rang through to answering machines or silence. The ones who answered listened to an awkward mix of apology, insistence, and hesitation worthy of a telemarketer on her first day. A few were hostile, one worked out a payment plan, and another announced that she could pay in full. Ebenezer figured the last would buy her a few more days to job search, at least.

She had been avoiding Martha Cratchit's number since two-thirty. At six, the thought of putting it off any longer became as miserable as it was unfeasible. Ebenezer's fingers trembled as the computer dialed and the phone rang hollowly.

"Hello."

The script felt like a cactus in her throat.

"Hello?" A huff punctuated the salutation. "Ebenezer, look. I know it's you, just like you know I don't have a penny more'n I did yesterday and cussing me out won't make it come no faster. Bye."

"No!" Ebenezer gasped. "Don't hang up. Please? I'm not going to call again."

She listened for a dial tone.

"What?" Martha asked instead.

"I'm not going to call again," Ebenezer said evenly, but with some trepidation. "And I've been a real bitch to you this month." A furtive glance left revealed a blond head bent to a computer screen; a glance right showed an empty cubicle. So far, so good.

Martha cleared her throat, sounding more taken aback than annoyed.

"Well. Yeah. So, what's the game now? You going to play nice to squeeze blood from a stone instead? By the way," she said before Ebenezer could answer, "no cops came over Christmas Eve. You forget to call them, or did they tell you to quit harassing sick old women?"

"That's what they would have said, if I'd called." Ebenezer checked right and left again. "Martha...Mrs. Cratchit, there are no police. There never were. No warrant, either, or anything else I told you."

"Yeah." Martha sighed. "Whatever you say, little girl. But that's not really the point. Point is, you people call me all day long, tie up the phone, make my two little kids cry, send my blood pressure through the ceiling. Do you have any idea what harm you do?"

Trent swept past her cubicle, two steaming coffee mugs in hand, sporting his usual shark-sharp smile.

Ebenezer blanched and swiveled back to her computer screen as she ducked her head.

"I know, I know," she whispered when he was out of earshot. "I've done something terrible to you, and I'm sorry. I don't expect you to forgive me, but I just...I hope you'll let me try to help.

"I don't know. I can't help you pay back the hospital. I wish...I really wish I could." When Martha offered no objection, she struggled on, her voice hardly cracking. "But the only thing I know how to do is say you have options. Payment plans, debt consolidation. You can even tell us to send you everything in writing. So no more phone calls."

Ebenezer gritted her teeth into a nervous smile as Martha breathed heavily, in and out like tides.

"Fine. But if you're lying to me, I swear to God...!"

As quietly and quickly as she could, Ebenezer whispered the necessary steps while making note of Martha Cratchit's insistence on postal-only contact. How many people she would be able to offer similar advice before getting caught was a guess she could not begin to hazard.

"That's how it works," she concluded ten minutes later.

Martha responded with a grunt that could have indicated anything from thankfulness to murderous intent.

"Mrs. Cratchit," Ebenezer tried, "this year has... things have been bad for a long time, for a lot of people. Everyone I know. I hope life will, um, turn around for you soon."

"Yeah, thanks a lot," Martha grumbled. "It's been swell." And the line went dead.

As the computer disconnected, Ebenezer dug her toes into the carpet and noticed that she was both trembling and blushing. But the twisting in her stomach made her even more uncomfortable. When she had wished Martha well, she had meant it—and advice coupled with easy platitudes would not be enough.

No one had ever accused Ebenezer of meddling—it was one of a dozen new temptations. But she had seen Martha's family. She had seen Claire. Turning away felt not only cruel but impossible—yes, both. She had rarely felt so sure of anything.

"All right there, Ebenezer?"

All three hundred pounds of Fred Carter grinned from the entrance to her cubicle, and Ebenezer had only noticed him on the second repetition.

"Oh," she said, swiveling her chair around. "Sorry, Fred. I guess I was distracted. But, yes. I'm all right." And this time when she smiled it felt weaker than a shadow but certainly genuine. She wondered if her supervisor would notice.

When he returned her smile with the same awkward, confused look, she knew he must have.

"Well, that's wonderful! I'm glad to hear it! Did you have a good Christmas?"

"Something like that." It seemed like the best answer. "And did you and Carl have fun?"

Fred's smile wavered just a little as Ebenezer realized her mistake.

"Um. Yes, we had dinner and watched old movies. I told you about him?"

"Last week, I think." Ebenezer shrugged off the lie and grabbed onto the first topic change that came to mind. "The candy cane."

"Hm?"

"The one you gave me on Christmas Eve. I wasn't really—I had a lot on my mind this Christmas, so I didn't have your gift with me."

Fred beamed as if she had just given him the moon.

"Oh, there's no need. Knowing you had a good holiday is enough. More than enough."

And the damned thing was, she knew he really meant that.

"No, there is," she pressed. "It isn't much, but I thought I'd get you lunch today. Or later, if you brought your own. I'd say coffee but...I don't drink it, either."

"Well, I wouldn't want you to spend so much..." But Ebenezer knew Utah politeness would win out, given five seconds. "Okay. How does an early dinner sound? I'm off at six today, too. The Thai place across the way is good."

"Thai place." Ebenezer nodded.

As Fred departed with an 80-watt goodbye, the second guesses started. Did he think this was a come-on? And, more important, why a dinner? What could she possibly say for half an hour a nice card wouldn't cover in less personal and more eloquent terms?

He had looked so sad on Christmas Eve.

For the rest of her shift, Ebenezer restlessly turned through her call lists, trying to ignore the idea. But with each call, it only grew in strength. If she couldn't help Martha, she would help Fred. Or try to. If he wanted it. She hoped he did. She hoped she could. As the minutes vanished on the computer clock, Ebenezer felt as giddy as a child, and terrified as a baby.

As it turned out, Fred had some last-minute work to do, so Ebenezer had time to worry her way through two shrimp-stuffed spring rolls and half a pot of jasmine tea, neither of which she could afford, although for once she didn't care if she ate ramen for the rest of her life to pay for it. She had almost forgotten how bracing real food could be, even if it did come on a chipped plate with a faded border of mimosas.

As she ordered a bowl of Pad Thai from the black-haired waitress, a clatter of bells interrupted the faint murmur of pop tunes on the overhead speakers. The restaurant was now deserted save for her, two waiters slurping oily tom yam in a corner, and now Fred, draping his charcoal wool coat across the back of his chair.

"Sorry about that. Trent had to talk to me for a minute there. I hope you got an appetizer or something."

Ebenezer nodded and hid her frown in her teacup; fifty percent of his smile have been siphoned away.

"No problem." She shrugged, pushing the menu across the table. "The spring rolls are really good. So is the green curry."

The grin flickered back, to her relief.

"I see you're a connoisseur." And when the waitress glided over he requested both.

"Well, I guess so. I used to eat here all the time with Marley."

"Marley?" Fred turned his water glass in one great hand, his brow furrowed as if he had just spotted a stain.

"My ex-girlfriend." She could say it almost without a wince.

He lowered the glass without outcry.

"Oh," he said neutrally. And then: "I'm sorry—that is, if I should be."

239

"Thank you. It wasn't the best breakup." Ebenezer swirled her tea as a laugh broke from her lips. "Wow. I invited you, and here I am, wrecking it."

"You didn't wreck anything," Fred insisted. "I can't say as I'll understand too well—I just don't know that many gay people. But if you need to talk about her, I'll listen."

"How did you get into this business?"

The question's abruptness made them both blink.

"Into collections, right?" Fred asked at last. "Well, let's just say history teachers aren't exactly in the kind of high demand the college recruiters thought. Or more like I imagined, I guess."

"Why not sell books or make coffee?" Ebenezer pressed. "Or work at a museum. They must need people."

"I thought so, too."

Ebenezer stared down into the teacup's steam.

"I'm sorry. I should mind my own business."

"No, you're fine." But Fred's smile dropped into a melancholy grimace. "The truth is, sometimes life takes you places, and you just get stuck there."

"Yeah, that sounds familiar."

Fred thanked the waitress as she delivered his water.

"How about you?" he asked when she had gone. "You got your degree in—I'm guessing theatre?"

"Acting. Like history, only with fewer job prospects." Ebenezer shrugged. "And just as much sticking potential."

Fred turned his to gaze out the window, where snow was falling like bone dust.

"Why do you think we did it?" he asked after a while.

"The same reason anybody gets stuck. We were afraid. And we still are. Plus, you know, a salary. Health insurance."

Ebenezer did not turn away when he looked back at her, or when that smiling mouth twitched into a question she suspected he had wanted to ask for quite some time.

"You really are unhappy there, aren't you?"

"Yes. I am. Are you?" Her pulse beat softly in her palms, which were not even clammy as she asked it.

"Yes. I am."

Before both could drift like snow into shock or silence, their food arrived on more scratched and haphazard plates, and there was the business of missing chopsticks and a refilled teapot to contend with—time in which Ebenezer considered what to say next. No words, however, had conjured themselves by the time she dug her fork into the sticky noodles.

"It's just—" Fred started.

"It's just all the yelling. Sorry, go on."

"No, you. Please."

They smiled grimly at each other then laughed nervously, like conspirators.

"Really," Fred insisted.

"Well…it's just that I hate taking things from people—and money. Especially from people who don't have it, through no fault of their own."

"I know. We're supposed to treat the poor right, and forgive people their debts. That's what I learned at Primary, anyway. God, all that corporate nonsense."

241

"And the tactics. All that threatening..."

"Having to tell your people to call over and over, even though the answer's not going to change any time soon. No matter what Trent says."

"You think it's hard for actors and history teachers to find work? It's even worse for land sharks. I mean, really, Fred. What else can he do? Or Cynthia?"

"Land sharks, huh? You're probably right. Regular sharks wouldn't have 'em." He chuckled. "That's a good one. You're really funny. And it's good to laugh about this sometimes."

"Yeah, I guess so. After awhile it just sucks you dry."

"Yeah." Fred sighed. "Yeah, it does." He stirred his curry with a familiar kind of leaded thoughtfulness. "Well, what now?"

"I don't know," Ebenezer admitted. "At least there have to be telemarketing jobs and collection jobs that aren't like this. Maybe we could even look together. I mean, two heads, right?"

"History teachers and actors probably need at least a few more than that." Fred blew across a steaming piece of broccoli. "Well, at least we've got some time to look."

"Yeah, about that..." Ebenezer fidgeted with her napkin as she explained what she had done during her shift. By the time she finished, the paper was a mess of tatters and Fred's smile had sunk several fathoms.

"Oh. Well. I guess that *is* a problem. Or it would be if I'd heard you say that. Phew," and he gulped down half of his water in seconds. "You didn't warn me this was spicy."

Ebenezer felt like hugging him. The thought of physical contact was not nearly as terrifying as the one that had been forming during their conversation—and, if she was honest, since her strange trip the night before. She fished through her noodles for awhile, as if the best way to say it might be hidden in the sauce.

"I have a friend. I mean, one who knows, well, like everybody. She might—no promises—but she might know someone who's looking. I'll ask her. Maybe she can help."

It was a good excuse, but still an excuse. Ebenezer was thankful the dinner conversation then strayed to the subject of her mother and then Carl, to Utah and its changing seasons, to the city university that had signed both of their degrees, although several years apart.

When they parted, the snow still looked like broken glass, and the noodles felt like worms inside her stomach as she turned her collar up against the evening.

Bell.

Scene IV

As Good a Friend

Bell.

More than Ronelle, Marley—hell, even more than Trent or Cynthia or any of the geniuses—Ebenezer feared seeing her. Each block to the subway brought her only a patter of reassurances that crumbled like newspaper in the rain.

Of all the people in her life, Bell was the most likely to forgive, and even more likely to understand, a multitude of failures, omissions, even outright slights. At the very least, she would be kind.

She would be kind.

Ebenezer had a reason for visiting—to talk about work. *To talk about work.* She repeated it like an affirmation with each footstep. To talk about work. To ask for help. Both familiar things. Both easy. Yet, her words to New York City kept rolling back down on her.

She wants to be my friend.

Of all the things she had witnessed in the past two days, Ebenezer felt certain nothing had terrified her more.

The subway's abandoned periodicals, including a forgotten issue of *Backstage*, could not distract her from

244

the trembling in her limbs. She clutched her hands in her lap and tried to make her mind go blank as the dim subterranean walls slid past like gravestones—a thought that made her queasy and anxious to look elsewhere.

By the time she stepped off the subway in Cobble Hill, Ebenezer was a mess of nerves, sweat, and bad storytelling. As she trudged through the sludge and the unfamiliar, darkened brownstone-lined streets, she entertained the desperate hope of getting lost—preferably until fatigue and weather drove her back onto a Manhattan train.

Unfortunately, Bell's apartment building was only two blocks east of the subway entrance, and Ebenezer had not forgotten the weathered red brick from the times Marley had forced her to visit.

"Turning back is not an option," she repeated several times before closing her eyes and jamming a knuckle against the buzzer.

When the speaker failed to click on immediately, Ebenezer was sure she had missed her—the day after Christmas, yes, but wouldn't Bell's social calendar be inked up, nonetheless?

"Hello."

Ebenezer jumped as Bell's voice came through, although a bit throatier than usual.

"Uh…" She rubbed her sweaty palms against her coat. "Uh. Hi. Bell. It's—it's Ebenezer."

Bell sniffled thickly, but the tone of her voice was bright enough.

"Oh, yeah! Hey! Merry Christmas."

On second thought, this sounded like the aftereffects of tears. Ebenezer balked—had Bell been crying? The notion immediately filled her with rage and brick-heavy guilt.

"I'm sorry. Did I come at a bad time?"

"Hm? Oh. No!" Bell blew her nose. "Sorry. Just a rough day. So, you wanna come in and have some tea or something? Coffee? Let me buzz you up."

And just like that, the door buzzed.

A squeaky—and in her opinion, interminable—elevator ride later, Ebenezer found the door to Bell's apartment unlocked and just as heavy and baby-puke green as she remembered. The studio's interior, however, could not have been more different.

What appeared at first glance to be clutches of flowers were actually piles of colorful cloth arranged in all stages of neatness and clutter. The tops and innards of every bookshelf played home to masks, hats, and a number of large and unclassifiable costume pieces in a similar state. The dull light peeking in between the blinds threw a headless Victorian wire dummy and its sleek green dress into such breathtaking relief that Ebenezer fleetingly wished she had a camera.

"Bell?" she called, not seeing the room's occupant, and blushed when it came out in a squeak.

"Over here."

Ebenezer pivoted to find Bell seated behind an industrial sewing machine. From her flutter-sleeved dress of black crushed velveteen to the magenta tips of her spiked hair, she looked impeccable—even beautiful. Her eyelids, however, looked bloated from what Ebenezer guessed was at least a night of crying. Had the party soured after her departure? Enough to affect her a day later?

But when Ebenezer waved, Bell's world-embracing smile was warm enough.

"Well, this is a surprise. Didn't think you were really one for house calls." Bell winked and stood up heavily, her bosom swelling as she stretched her shoulders back. "Tea's on. Sit anywhere you can find a seat, and sorry for the mess—I got a show opening in five weeks, and a director that can't make up her mind on anything except she doesn't know what the hell she wants, but it isn't anything I've showed her yet. You know the type."

A whistle from a semi-clear stretch of table cut off her patter; Bell wove through the well-choreographed mess to a tabletop where a striped electric tea kettle steamed.

"You like chamomile? Peppermint? Green? Some mystery herbal thing, because I lost the label on the tin?" Her laughter carried a touch of nervousness Ebenezer could not remember having heard before.

"Peppermint's fine." Ebenezer settled on a rickety plush sofa between two bolts of what appeared to be, from right to left, blue taffeta and black rayon shot through with holographic sparkles.

"Sugar? Honey?"

Ebenezer lurched up.

"What?"

"For the tea?"

"Oh. Um. Plain's fine." She shifted on the cushions, uncomfortable for more reasons than the bolts pressing against her slender thighs.

Bell's hands noticeably trembled as she dropped too many sugar cubes into her own pink mug.

"We missed you Christmas Eve," she said over a shoulder. "After midnight, things just became one great big sugar rush. Angel Moroni won the cage fight against Santa and Krampus. I thought of you." The tears broke through her voice like an ice pick. "B–best party ever, I think."

Turning around, she wiped her forearm across her eyes as she pulled a ball of tissues from a pocket.

"Don't mind me, okay? Just some bad news when we were cleaning up and some weird dream-thing that night that just won't go the fuck away—real lovely stuff."

Only a handful of days ago, Ebenezer knew she would have changed the subject to any number of inappropriate things. But the past had moved so very far away now that for a few moments, she could not even recall her initial reason for stopping in.

"Bell, what is it? What's the matter?"

"Oh, you know." The seamstress flopped one large hand dismissively. "The usual New York City drama. You throw a party, and one friend says he can't come. There's family stuff." She shrugged. "Turns out that stuff involved *nearly* jumping off a bridge while having a psychotic break." She looked down at her knuckles then, which had gone bloodless from their grip on the table's edge. "Fuck. Oh, fuck. I'm sorry. I think I need to sit down. Can you…?" She gestured feebly to her sewing chair.

"Sure. Sure." In a few strides, Ebenezer had steered her back into it and fetched her mug of tea.

"Just push the damned patterns off the bed," Bell told her before she could return to the sofa. "God knows, I'm not getting anything done with them today. Sheena's probably going to hate them, anyway. So what's the fucking point?"

All the same, Ebenezer moved the papers gently to the floor before perching delicately near Bell's pillows. She found her hand on top of Bell's before she knew that she had moved it.

"What can I do? I mean—it's stupid. I know how stupid that sounds. But I mean it. If there's anything. Food, or if you want someone to just…" She could hardly believe what she was saying, yet there it was.

Bell looked up from her tea and met her gaze. For a moment, neither woman moved.

"Just someone to talk to?" She patted Ebenezer's knuckles with her free hand. "Remember when I introduced you to Tim?"

With just a twinge of guilt, Ebenezer said that she did not.

Bell frowned.

"Huh. That's weird." But then she shrugged off the thought. "Sweet guy. Wall Street grunt, the kind they don't pay shit, but you'd never know it with how much time he spends on Broadway. Plays piano, dabbles in poetry, and cooks on Sundays. Great wife and kids. You know, all the things you think make someone stable, until you realize they're not. Until they wander out onto the Brooklyn Bridge on Christmas fucking Eve and do something so…Not stupid. I shouldn't say stupid. Desperate."

She bit her lip and shook her head.

"Ann doesn't know how he got home—that's his wife," she said. "Because *he* doesn't know. He thinks that…that someone put him in a cab and…" She shook her head.

Ebenezer felt her stomach knot. The last thing she wanted to do now or ever was explain to Bell exactly who had put Tim into that car or what had driven it.

"Oh. That's...uh..."

"It's just confusing. He's confused," Bell decided for her. "When he calms down, he'll probably tell us more. Or not. I don't know." She wiped her broad palm down her face. "I just don't know. It sucks. You know?"

"I know." Ebenezer shifted back onto the pillows. "My mom made about twelve attempts before I graduated college."

Bell's jaw did not drop immediately, and her hands were not fast enough to hold back a gasp.

"Oh, my God. I am so sorry."

Ebenezer waved a hand dismissively.

"Don't be. I mean, thank you. But she's stable now. And you learn to deal. As fucked up as it sounds."

Bell nodded. "I wish you'd told me. Not because I have to know everything about my friends, especially when they're painful things. But because I would have listened."

"It's not something I like to talk about most of the time." Ebenezer looked down at her hands. "Who am I kidding? I don't like to talk about *anything* most of the time."

"Yeah. I'd kind of noticed that." But Bell was smiling, small but genuine. "You know what? Fuck it. The point is he didn't go through with it. He's getting help. He'll be okay." She blew across the surface of her tea. "As okay as any of us, anyway.

"Wow. Listen to me. Here I'm going on about some guy, and you've had a holly fucking jolly season. How about a subject change?" Blowing her nose one last time, she scooted her chair closer to the bed. "How are you doing? You okay?"

"Okay as any of us."

"I tried to call Christmas Eve. You know, as a reminder, just in case, with all the weirdness lately."

"I'm sorry about that."

Bell gave her a wide-eyed look as she gulped her tea.

"Why? Don't be! I know how much Marley meant to you. Means to you. Love's not like a light bulb; you don't just turn it off or change what you feel because some people think it should be easy. Or because it's Christmas. I just called in case you wanted to get out for awhile. And, you know…watch a giant menorah beat up a Christmas tree."

Ebenezer's chuckle ended abruptly as Bell's fingers swept over her shoulder.

"I'm here for you, okay? Whatever you need. It's what friends do."

"I haven't been a very good friend to you, though."

"Eh. Good thing that's easily fixed, huh? I mean that, by the way. I want us to be better friends."

Ebenezer felt far too dried out to cry again, but a lump rose in her throat all the same.

"Ebenezer? Have we lost you?"

"There is something you can do."

Bell stared at her dumbly, saying only, "Yeah?"

"I hate my job!" And she told her everything she had told Fred, although in terms far more passionate and colorful. "So I know…I know I don't have any right to ask, because I've been so distant and…"

251

"Oh, will you stop, already?! You're sounding like my mother." Bell tapped her lightly on the nose. "Of course I'll help. A year ago would have been a better time, but I'll ask around. Don't worry. It might be a piddly little job in a pizza place for a while, but we'll find something for you and Fred—who, by the way, needs to come to one of my parties. I highly recommend Not-Valentine's. There's going to be cake and burlesque involving cake. Marley and Yuri are even going out of town for the weekend—you probably know who that is by now."

"The weird thing is, I don't think it's going to bother me for very long."

"Huh." Bell nodded thoughtfully. "Not that you need to hurry up, remember, but it's good not to be jealous. Believe me, I know." She looked like she wanted to say something else, but in the end she simply asked, "So, what did it?"

"Hm?"

"The thing is, when I met you however long ago, I knew you weren't very happy with your job. With life, either. I'm sorry. It was just one of those things people have to figure out, or I'd have said something then. But I was also just this strange person you'd just met on the job, and it felt sort of presumptuous—which I, of course, have never been." She winked. "Seriously, what was the last nose in the camel's straw, or whatever? Was there even one, or just a mountain of bullshit?"

"You really want to know?"

"Nooo! I just asked to get us to stop being so damn weepy!" Bell made a face.

Ebenezer flopped back on the bed.

"You're going to hate me."

"Before I graduated and the sewing, radio commercial, pouring chocolate-flavored lube in my hair onstage to be artsy gig, I paid for what the scholarship didn't cover by working night shifts at a diner. After what I saw there, I don't think I could hate anyone—unless you've been flinging shit around restrooms like a monkey." The mattress creaked as Bell sat down beside her and gave her a long, mock-serious look. "You haven't fucked up any restrooms, right?"

"Nope."

"Or left three pennies for some poor waitress cuz she didn't bring you a Sprite in less than two-point-thirty-seven seconds?"

Ebenezer chuckled. "Can't say I did that, either."

"All right, then. Pope Bell the First hereby absolves you of any sins, past, present, and future—so long as you meant that about tips." She pressed her thumb onto Ebenezer's nose. "Beep."

Ebenezer doubted she had truly grinned in years. She wasn't surprised when her face strained with the effort.

"It's actually not really funny."

"No, I didn't think so. I thought I'd give you a warmup."

"Heh." The actress stared up at the ceiling for a moment, mapping the outlines of the glow-in-the-dark stars and planets affixed there. "There's this family...a lot of families, probably, but this one in particular. They live right across from Tim, too, actually."

Ebenezer's eyes had closed with shame, so she didn't notice as Bell's expression widened in shock, or how it settled down as she told the story—or as much of it as she could tell without meandering into details she could have gleaned only from a night walking at a spirit's side.

"Mhm," Bell chorused thoughtfully from time to time. "Mhm," she murmured again when Ebenezer had concluded. "Yeah, that's pretty evil. But since you have to pay the bills, too, it's more like evil Olestra—just shit for everyone. So, you were the one bugging Tim's neighbors. And people say New York City's too big."

"I want to make it up to them."

"Other than saying sorry and slipping them that cheat sheet, I think that boat's pretty much sailed."

Ebenezer hadn't sensed the idea's presence in her mind's dank chambers until it sprang from her mouth, fully formed and carrying a shield.

"No." She raised up on her elbows. "No, I meant more like a fundraiser."

The expression on her face, she realized, must have been very surprised and very strange, because Bell's matched it for a moment…and then melted into a full-bodied laugh.

"That's really—"

"Stupid? Presumptuous?"

Bell rolled her eyes.

"No, more like get out of my brain. That's what I'd have said, too. Only there's no way they have the time or energy to pull something like that off alone. How much did you say Martha owed again?"

"Fifty thousand."

Bell's lips pursed as she rubbed her spiky hair.

"Difficult. But possible—in increments. If we call in the whole fucking cavalry. Maybe." She tapped her fingers against her teeth, considering. "The Chapman people love me, and I love them. So we might have a space there for a night."

"A night?"

"A performance!"

"So, like, let's put on a show and save the homestead from the bill collectors?" Ebenezer raised her eyebrows.

"It's what we do," Bell said gravely. "Well, besides putting things up on eBay and donating plasma." Snapping her fingers, she climbed from the bed and began pacing the room. "Okay. How's this? Forget the Not-Valentine's party? We'll do a thing instead. Like open mic—no!"

She turned so fast she toppled a pile of bolts.

"An open performance!" she cried, completely ignoring them. "With a twist. We charge people a pay-whatever price to get in, and a set price to perform, like five bucks each minute. And we give everybody a theme and ask them to make a piece around it, a song, a skit, whatever—based on *Casablanca*, maybe, or *Tristan und Isolde*, or *Romeo and Juliet*…"

Ebenezer had chosen that unfortunate moment to sip her tea and nearly choked.

"Excuse me?"

"You know, something obvious and Valentine's and hetero-normative!"

"And…this would raise money?"

Bell laughed. "Do you know how much a shit-load constitutes, Ebenezer? The address book in my fucking Gmail account for work! And you know who makes up that shitload, Ebenezer? Not just performers, but Wall Street types that aren't low-paid grunts! We could even extend this to three nights, if we can pay the overhead, the electricity..."

"It's amazing."

Bell blinked. "Sorry, now I'm the one saying 'excuse me.'"

"You are. I mean—when you're, um, thinking up something like this. It's kind of...I've never seen you do it before, I guess, so it's kind of..."

"Intimidating?" Bell prompted. "Most people who see me do this call it scary in a good way, so that's also a good answer."

"Well, they're right."

"I'm not saying it'll work out, of course. Fifty thousand is a lot of money. But we've got to try something, right? So it might as well be this if we can put it together. Besides, if Tim gets out by party time, he'll probably want something to distract himself—and he's hilarious when he gets on stage. And of course, you'll also be delighting us again, right?"

Ebenezer just stared at her.

"Well, I'm sort of out of practice..."

"Do I have to tell you again how brilliant your improv is? Because I will. Come on. If this works out, will you act?"

Her answer meant getting hurt again, being angry and being disappointed. In the end, though, Ebenezer found that it terrified her far less than the other choice.

"Yes."

Bell actually clapped her hands with childlike enthusiasm.

"Ebenezer, I promise this is not me finding a new way to freak out after being up all Christmas night crying and comforting Ann, and freaking out all yesterday—even though it kind of is—but I am just kvelling here."

"It isn't like anyone will notice that I'm going to act again," Ebenezer said.

"Tim will notice. Marley will notice. My friends will notice. Everyone at the party will notice. I'll notice." Bell pouted.

"I guess that's true." Ebenezer massaged her temples. She had always found Bell's energy anything from trying to annoying, but now it felt like sunlight over a granite statue, like the bit of spring that kicks beneath the ribs long before the first buds shiver off their ice.

It was also kind of charming, she mused. Not to mention cute.

"Okay, then," Bell said, plopping back down onto the bed. "So now you know you're not a bad actress, along with not only being not evil, but maybe an angel."

The last word snapped Ebenezer from her reverie.

"I'm sorry. What?"

"Can I ask you something weird? You don't know Tim, right?"

Ebenezer shook her head.

"'Kay, here's what I don't understand. When Ann found him outside the door, he didn't say too much that made sense. Things about spirits, shaking chains, rivers. The weird thing, though? Is that Ann was almost more upset by the fact he said a woman in a taxi brought him home."

"Oh." Ebenezer coughed, hoping the sound could cover up her pounding heart.

"Well, not about *that*. They're the most in-love old couple I've ever met. 'But Ebenezer's not a woman's name,' she said. I mean, there's probably *women*—especially from Utah, where they think Trelis and Desdedididawn look great on birth certificates. And as nosy as debt collectors are, I don't think they know everybody's neighbors."

"Not really," Ebenezer tried. "We call them all the time, just like we call bosses."

"What's his last name?"

Ebenezer could only offer a blank look.

Bell nodded. "Ebenezer, look. You say you're doing okay, but if you were on that bridge trying to do the same thing, you two are going to just kill me. And because I really don't want to spend the new year dead, or either of you to spend it dead, you'll let me be nosy just this one time, right?"

"Marley and I used to go there all the time." It was true. "So I was just there, thinking."

"In the middle of a snowstorm."

"People do weird things when they're grieving."

"I know. So what's the real story?"

Ebenezer shut her eyes again as she considered any number of lies that would make her sound at least halfway honest. In the end, all of them made her feel sick, as sick as she had felt the last six years. *Go forward*, the Genius of the Future had insisted. And how, the actress thought, could she do that by lying to someone who had never been anything but honest with her?

She sighed and turned her gaze to Bell, who was waiting patiently, but with her large hands planted firmly on her hips.

"All right. But you're going to think I'm lying. Or that I really do need help."

"Two weeks ago, a grown woman paid me an obscene sum of money to dress a dozen fourteen-year-olds up like Elder Gods for something called "Beth's Eldritch Birthday Bash." Actually paid me. After that, nothing would surprise me."

Ebenezer swallowed. "After this, I sort of think you will. If I said I spent Christmas Eve with the spirits of Utah, New York City, and the Future, what would you say?"

"That I either want whatever you were drinking or a subscription to your newsletter. Or, at least, more details."

Once again, Ebenezer found herself thrust into a story, only this time one that made her feel vulnerable and, strangely, far too young. But as she blushed and stumbled her way through, Bell sat patiently, asking questions, prompting her when she stalled.

Of course, most of it felt too personal, or at least too fresh, but she managed the highlights—Utah's warmth, the night jaunts through the city, even the breathing hourglass and the tomb that had nearly consumed her—although she spared Bell a recount of her skills as a funeral organizer.

"Hm," Bell offered when she had finished.

"Does that 'hm' mean 'I believe you,' or 'hm, you're obviously developing an anxiety disorder?'"

"Well, you and the rest of the world there. But stranger things have happened. Like waking up at five a.m. on Christmas morning with you looking through the mirror at me."

Ebenezer could not be sure, exactly, but from the feel of it, every single hair above her waist was now standing at attention

"I tried to sleep about two hours before I said fuck it and started putting together that dress by the window. I was—it was supposed to be ready at the party, but clearly that didn't happen. So it was a good excuse not to keep thrashing around like a schmuck.

"I don't know what happened. Maybe I saw something moving or maybe I heard something. But I looked up at the mirror on the wall, and there was your face. Sure, it scared the shit out of me—for a second. Then I just thought I was tired and stressed out, which I was. But when I blinked, and you were still there, I was…" She held her hands out like two scales.

"You were?" Ebenezer whispered.

"What can I say? I smiled like an asshole. Because you looked happier than I had ever seen you. Like whatever you've been carrying since I first met you had just slid off your back. That's a stupid simile, but I don't know how else to describe it. And I just…you don't want to hear this part."

"Why?"

"Because it's the last thing you need right now."

"I spent Christmas Eve with a super-sized model of the Statue of Liberty that swore at me. I didn't need *that*, either. But I'm here."

Bell nodded before looking down into her lap.

"I was reaching out for you and saying your name like you could hear me, like this sort of thing just hap-

260

pened every day. I wasn't close enough, though, and I missed your face by, like, this much." She held a pinch of air between her fingers. "You were gone before I could try again." Bell's fingers fisted into the bed's mauve sheets as she whispered, low as wind, "Do you see? I wanted to touch you. Do you see?"

And finally, Ebenezer did. As their hands twined together, Bell's head snapped up from its low bow.

"You were wrong, you know. I needed that. And you didn't miss."

Both of their hands trembled as they squeezed and held.

"I swear to God. This holiday's going to kill me." Bell snorted as she wiped her eyes again. "So, what now?"

"Well, I can't really think of anything."

"No. You were going to say, 'What I really wanted for Christmas was a little green dress!' And I was going to say, 'How strange! I was just making one.'" Bell indicated the dummy with a nod. "And since I fucked up the timing, that it was now going to be a New Year's gift, because, well, the new year should be beautiful. Especially after this one."

"It's lovely." Ebenezer's fingers glided across the fabric. "Soft."

"I have absolutely no idea if it fits. But when you have time, I thought I could fit it. Um. Professionally speaking, of course. It's getting late, so maybe this weekend?"

Ebenezer glanced at the clock.

"Nine-thirty isn't late, especially when you work evenings. Is now a good time?

"Well, my schedule was obscenely clear tonight. Bathroom's behind the bookshelf. Just ignore the tub filled with sewing crap." She unzipped the garment and pulled it up over the dummy's wire bust. "Like any Bellwether creation, this dress has a little bit of magic sewn into its lining—unless you wear it to an audition at least once a month, it turns into a pumpkin."

"I'll try and remember." Ebenezer smirked as she took it up into her arms.

Before she could shut the bathroom door, Bell called out, "Hey."

"Yes?"

"Merry Christmas, Ebenezer."

"Merry not-Christmas." And as Ebenezer shut the door, a prayer sprung to her lips for the first time in her memory.

"God help us all."

Epilogue

The End of It

That Christmas Eve was not the last time Ebenezer had dealings with spirits. As the red canyons, streets, and cemeteries of the world are haunted, so, too, are the people who walk within them—haunting, of course, being nothing but a lesson forgotten or a habit resurfaced. In time, she came to view the geniuses of past, present, and future not as arrows to flee but as dear friends urging her forward, sometimes cheering, sometimes pushing, but never passive or allowing her to become so again.

Or, at least, not quite as passive she had been in her youth. And while life was seldom what she hoped, it was—thankfully, beautifully—life, nonetheless.

But, Ebenezer thought as she bowed low before the packed house and wild applause at Bell's Not-Valentine's Day Party But Fuck You Broken Health-care System Fuckers Extravaganza with Light Entertainment, life was not exactly what she had feared, either.

In the front row, Ronelle clapped and shifted her daughter—Ebenezer's niece—into Nikolai's arms so she could stand. Hand-in-hand, Tim and Ann followed her up, then Fred, Nikolai, Clea, Carl, and Right from her former place of employment, whom Ebenezer now knew as Monica.

She smiled and nodded at them before turning her head to look at Bell, who grinned and mouthed what appeared to be *Ten thousand*.

As of yesterday, Bell had counted nearly five thousand dollars in donations, so, Ebenezer thought, the three-day run had worked out better than expected.

Really? she mouthed back.

Bell's lips clearly said *yes*—and, of course she would know, Ebenezer thought as she watched the ostentatious pink light shift across Bell's tattoo. She often told the seamstress that the design reminded her of someone different, depending on mood, lighting, and sometimes even the weather. Sometimes it looked like Utah's smiling face, sometimes like New York City's sneer, sometimes like Marley's or Tim's, sometimes like Melora's, Clea's, Hector's or any number of the faces in the dim audience whose names she was slowly learning, slowly saying, slowly savoring.

She had been through a twenty-nine-year winter, Ebenezer decided as she bowed again and blew a kiss. But now, if she just turned her head and listened a bit, she could almost hear it—the future looming up, unwritten but no longer empty.

Ebenezer laughed, and knew she heard the city beyond the black box's walls rumble a laugh back. She was performing. And it was enough.

END

About the Author

JOSELLE VANDERHOOFT is an author, editor, poet, journalist, with a passion for LGBTQ books—especially the LB and T. Her anthology *Steam-Powered: Lesbian Steampunk Stories* was a Lambda Literary Award finalist in 2012, and her co-edited anthologies *Hellebore & Rue* (with Catherine Lundoff) and *Heiresses of Russ 1* (with Steve Berman) finalists for the Golden Crown Literary Award, given annually for lesbian literature.

Her poetry has been nominated for the Rhysling Award and the 2008 Bram Stoker Award. Her other novel, *The Tale of the Miller's Daughter*, was released in 2006 and is scheduled to be reprinted soon.

Her other anthologies include more installments in the popular Steam-Powered series and the seventh volume of the popular WisCon Chronicles, which is scheduled for publication in 2013 and explores themes related to the convention, fandom, and disability. She is currently working on a trilogy of interlocking Cinderella stories tentatively titled *Transports of Delight* and a poetry collection about death in various world cultures.

A consummate fan of artisan perfume, yuri anime and manga, fairy tales, jewelry making, and anything to do with Doctor Who, Jo lives in South Florida with her partner, a beautiful orange tabby named Oscar, and a stray cat named Kia she'd like to adopt.

About the Artist

VANCE TRANCYGIER is a graphic designer and photographer from Salt Lake City, UT. He has created cover art for different publishing companies, including Drollerie Press and Redrum Horror.